THE KLONDIKE CAFE

CHINLE MILLER

For Roger

CONTENTS

1

Bud Shumway sat in the back booth of the Melon Rind Cafe, drinking coffee and pondering whether to drive up into Hondu Country and look for wild horses or maybe go on up to Bruin Point where he could probably get some photos of the aspen turning.

It was a difficult decision, Bud mused, but it was early, and he had plenty of time to decide. It was his day off as sheriff of Emery County, Utah, and his part-time deputy, Howie McPherson, was covering for him, not that there was much to cover in the little town of Green River.

There might be a few tourists passing through, some stopping by the melon stands to buy the town's most famous product—maybe its *only* product other than some alfalfa hay, Bud thought—but everything was slowing down now that autumn was here. And the melon farm Bud now owned with his wife, Wilma Jean, had been buttoned up and was sleepily waiting for the first snows to hit.

Bud knew bad weather could come at any time, though Green River usually had fairly mild winters, not getting much snow, mostly just sporadic winds. In any case, Bud felt a sense of contentment that things were ready for whatever may come, and he could now enjoy the Indian summer, wandering the countryside on his day off with his dogs and taking photos, his favorite activity.

Maureen, Deputy Howie's wife and the cafe's manager, refilled his cup, and Bud nodded his head in appreciation, then asked, "How are you feeling these days?"

She replied, "Not too bad, Bud. The baby's starting to kick, and sometimes that keeps me awake at night, but Howie just talks to him and he settles right back down."

"What does he say to him?" Bud asked.

"He just tells him all about astronomy stuff, you know, like stuff about the planets and stars and constellations and all that. Actually, I think maybe it puts *me* to sleep, to tell the truth."

Bud laughed. "Wilma Jean said you're interviewing for someone to help out here in the cafe."

Maureen replied, "I think we're going to hire Karen's daughter, Heather. She has lots of experience working at the Chow Down for her mom and will be here for the winter, taking some time off from school."

"Don't let her steal any recipes," Bud grinned. "Actually, maybe it would be good if she did, 'cause then when it's busy here I could go eat over there and get the same good food."

Maureen laughed, then turned her attention to the lanky man who'd just come into the cafe.

"Sit wherever you want," she said, handing him a menu.

The man sat in the booth across from Bud's, then looked around as if taking in all the details. Maybe he was writing a book or something, Bud thought.

The man reminded Bud of someone in the military with his short hair and no-nonsense appearance, his pale green shirt looking as if it had just been ironed and his tan cotton pants freshly creased. Bud couldn't see his shoes, but he suspected they were polished, a state that wouldn't last long in the little desert town.

After studying the menu, the fellow raised his hand as if in school, getting Maureen's attention, and asked, "Excuse me. I don't see it on the menu, which doesn't surprise me, but can I get you to make some poutine?"

Maureen's brow furrowed as she asked, "What's poutine?"

"Well," the man replied, "It's actually very easy to make, you just pour gravy over some cheese curds and fries."

"And it's called poutine? That's an odd name."

"Yes, it is, isn't it? I think maybe it's French for pudding, since it's from Quebec. I would be very grateful, and I'm sorry to put you to any trouble. I've just been craving poutine."

"Not a problem," Maureen replied. "Except for the curds. But I can do gravy on fries with cheese sprinkled on top. Is that all you want? Want some coffee or anything to drink?"

"Yes, coffee would be great, a double-double."

Bud was beginning to suspect that the man was far from being a local—maybe a good thousand miles or more, as in from Canada.

"What's a double-double?" Maureen asked.

"I'm sorry," the man replied. "It's two creams and two sugars."

"We let you do your own cream and sugar thing here," Maureen replied. "No offense, but fries, cheese, and gravy—how do you stay so trim?" Maureen now had her hand on her obviously pregnant midriff.

"I don't always eat like that," the man replied. "And I'm pretty active."

Maureen turned and went into the kitchen, and Bud wondered why the man would be in Green River, all the way from the North. Maybe he was just another tourist, but Bud suspected he was on some kind of business, as he didn't have the air about him of someone on vacation.

Bud asked congenially, "Missing your fine Canadian cuisine?"

The man, looking embarrassed, answered, "Poutine's too addictive. But I forget how different it is here."

Bud grinned, looking out the window at the small dusty town in the middle of the big sweeping desert he called the Big Empty. It seemed like it would be hard to forget how different it was from the green forests and mountains of the Great White North.

"I'll have to try the biscuits and gravy next time," the man said, again studying the menu. "Say, do you mind if I join you?"

Bud was surprised, but replied, "Sure, come on over."

Maureen had returned with a cup of coffee, following the man as he slipped into Bud's booth and placing the cup in front of him.

"I hope you don't think I'm being overly familiar," he said, adding cream and sugar to the cup. "This is my first time in the States, and maybe you can answer a few questions. I flew down and rented a car, so I've only been here a short time. My name's Dougald McDougald, but call me Dougie. That's pronounced Doo-gee, kind of like how you Yanks say Dougie, but with a Doo."

He held his hand out and shook with Bud.

"Nice to meet you, Dougie," Bud replied. "Bud Shumway."

"Nice meeting you, too. Can you recommend a place here to stay?"

Bud thought for a moment, then said, "Well, my wife has a nice B&B, if that's something you'd like."

"It depends on the cost," Dougie replied. "I have a per diem I have to adhere to."

Just then, Maureen put a plate of fries covered with hot steaming gravy and melted cheese in front of Dougie. As the aroma drifted to Bud, he decided he'd like a plate, too, and ordered one.

"I may have to put poutine on the menu," Maureen said.

"It has to have cheese curds to be real poutine," Bud said.

"And they have to be fresh, so you have to be near a dairy," Dougie added.

"Well, that lets us out," Bud grinned. "I'm not even sure where the nearest dairy is. But here's the number of the B&B—you can give them a call. You'll probably get Molly, the manager."

Bud wrote the number on a napkin, then added, "It's called Melon View, and I'm sure she can work with you on the price as things are pretty slow this time of year."

"Oh, that sounds nice. Is it in the country?" Dougie asked.

"It is, right by a watermelon field."

Maureen now sat a plate of fries, cheese, and gravy in front of Bud, saying, "Let me know how it is."

"It's delicious, in my opinion," Dougie replied, taking another bite. "Except it needs the cheese curds."

Bud now asked, "What part of Canada are you from, Dougie?"

Chewing for a moment, his mouth full of fries, Dougie finally said, "I'm originally from 'Berta, but I now live in Dawson City, Yukon Territory."

Bud whistled. "Alberta and Yukon Territory! Both are places I've always wanted to go. I would love to see the Canadian Rockies and the Northern Lights."

Dougie nodded his head, saying, "Yes, both are quite spectacular. But you have your own kind of beauty here, eh?" He gazed out the window as a tumbleweed drifted by.

Bud was surprised, not sure if Dougie was being sarcastic or not. Most saw the Big Empty as being just that, a big empty forsaken place. Only those who loved wide vistas and deep canyons really appreciated its beauty and unique desert landscape.

Dougie now turned back to Bud, asking, "Say, can you point me to the sheriff's office when we're done?"

Bud, surprised, said, "I can do better than that, I can point you to the sheriff himself."

Looking puzzled as Bud pointed at himself, Dougie then said, "Well, this is all too easy! I ask for poutine and almost get poutine, I immediately find a place to stay, and now I'm having lunch with the fellow I was sent here to see."

"You were sent to see me?" It was Bud's turn to be surprised.

Dougie leaned forward, making sure no one else could hear him, then said, "I'm with the RCMP, you know, the Royal Canadian Mounted Police, the Mounties. Surely you've heard of us?"

Bud answered quietly, "Of course, everyone's heard of the Mounties. You always get your man."

"We do, but this time, we've come to ask for your help in getting our man, though he's more like *your* man."

Bud sat his fork down as Dougie added, "Though it's always innocent until proven guilty, eh?"

Bud groaned. It appeared that his day off wandering with the dogs was quickly heading south—though unbeknownst to him, heading north would be more appropriate.

2

Bud sat at his big desk in the Emery County Sheriff's Office, wondering what poutine-flavored ice cream would taste like, waiting for Dougie to show up after going to check into a room at the Melon View B&B.

The fact that a Mountie had come all the way from the Yukon Territory to talk to him made Bud feel a bit unsettled, and he hoped it was something he could quickly get through so he could then get back to enjoying his day off.

He knew Deputy Howie was out on a call—someone over in the Palatial Estates Trailer Park had wanted to speak to an officer about lies in textbooks, and Howie had called Bud, asking what to tell them. Bud wasn't sure, so he'd told Howie to just wing it. Bud hadn't heard back, so he was curious as to what was going on.

Now Bud's thoughts went back to poutine-flavored ice cream, and he'd just decided that he would prudently stick to his old favorite of vanilla-bean when Wanda the mail carrier opened the door and placed a large envelope in front of him.

"You need to sign for this, Sheriff," she said in her no-nonsense manner. "It's registered, all the way from Canada."

"Canada?" Bud asked, surprised. "I don't know anyone in Canada."

He knew Wanda would want all the details, as she considered herself much more than just a simple mail carrier, but also the town's unofficial news carrier, since Green River didn't have a newspaper.

"You must know somebody up there or they wouldn't be sending you stuff," she replied, insinuating that Bud was withholding vital information. "It's from the Dawson Mining Recorder, 1242 Front Street, Dawson City, Yukon Territory, Y0B 1G0."

Not sure what to say, Bud signed the registered receipt, then stuck the envelope in his desk drawer, his instinct telling him this could be something he didn't want the entire town to know about, especially since a Mountie just coincidentally happened to be on his way for a visit.

"Thanks, Wanda," he replied. "I think this is an advertisement for selling gold claims. Seems like I saw something or other about it on the Internet. Some outfit's trying to sell off claims near where some gold-mining reality show was filmed, trying to capitalize on it."

"The Canadian Government?" Wanda asked suspiciously. "Seems like a mining recording office wouldn't get involved in something like that. And sending things registered is expensive."

Bud knew she was dying for him to open the envelope, but instead, he just said, "It's pretty common among scammers to make things sound official, and fake gold mines can pay off in big ways. I'll open it later. It's actually my day off."

He immediately regretted saying anything, for he knew Wanda would want to know why, if it was his day off, he wasn't out with his dogs, Hoppie and Pierre, but was instead hanging around the sheriff's office.

It seemed that Wanda knew exactly what everyone in town did on whichever or whatever day, and if they weren't doing exactly that, she wanted to know why. It was her way of making sure everything stayed orderly, at least in her own mind. Bud wondered if she might make a good deputy.

Bud now added, a bit lamely, "I'm just taking a break before I go get the dogs."

Wanda seemed satisfied with that, leaving just as Deputy Howie came through the door.

"Howdy, Sheriff," Howie said, grinning. "Boy, did I just get an earful from Mrs. Jensen."

"Mrs. Jensen? Why's that, Howie?" Bud asked.

"Well, I had to give her a ticket, Sheriff. She backed out of her driveway and hit a UPS truck. I saw the whole thing happen there at the trailer park. She was sure mad at the driver—she told him that she backs out every day and doesn't need to look. It was a pretty minor fender bender, but when I gave her the ticket, man, she sure turned the air blue, used words I've never heard before."

"And this is the same Mrs. Jensen who once filed a complaint when Old Man Green said hellsbells after she ran over him with her grocery cart at the Melon Harvest?"

"One and the same. She's also the one who called in about lies in textbooks, though we never got around to that."

"Probably for the best," Bud replied as Howie sat down.

"So what are you doing here on your day off, if you don't mind me asking?" Howie asked.

Bud sighed. "I'm here to meet a Canadian Mountie."

Howie was silent, then finally said, "Bud, I think you need a day off. Go on home and take a break."

Bud laughed. "I'm OK, Howie. I just met a fellow at the cafe, and he's on his way over here to talk to me. He's from Canada, a Mountie."

Howie whistled, then said, "I thought you were kidding. A real Mountie? What does he want? Did someone do something bad up North?"

"Well, they probably have people up there do bad things all the time, would be my guess," Bud replied. "People are pretty much the same everywhere."

Howie shook his head. "That's not what I meant, Sheriff. I mean, is he here looking for somebody?"

"I think so," Bud replied. "He pretty much said he was out to get his man, even though it was our man."

"Our man?" Howie asked. "We have someone who broke the law in Canada? Is he looking to extradite someone?"

"I think you could be on to something there, Deputy, but now you know as much about it as I do."

Howie whistled again, putting his feet up on Bud's desk, then quickly putting them back down, saying, "Someone's parking out front right now, Bud. Do you think he's looking for me?"

"Did you do something illegal in Canada?"

"Not that I recall," Howie replied. "I don't remember ever being there. But I think I'll go out on patrol."

Just then, Dougie came into the office, nodded at Bud, and introduced himself to Howie.

"I take it from your name tag that you're Deputy McPherson. I'm RCMP Sergeant Dougie McDougald. It's nice to meet you."

Howie stood, and they shook hands.

Just then, the phone rang.

"Emery County Sheriff, Bud speaking."

After a pause, Bud said, "I know, Mrs. Jensen, but you can't just go backing out without looking, even if you do it all the time. It *is* actually against the law, you know."

More silence, then Bud said, "Well, there's not much we can do about your insurance going up. And Deputy McPherson can't tear up that ticket. It's his job to enforce the law, Mrs. Jensen, but yes, I can send him back over to talk to you some more, if that's what you need. I'll have him bring the book that shows what you did was illegal."

Bud hung up and handed Howie a thick book from the nearby bookcase, all while shaking his head.

"I'm on it, Sheriff," Howie said, looking relieved as he hurried out the door.

"We have to stay ever alert here in the hinterlands," Bud said, turning to Dougie and smiling. "It's a tough job. Have a seat. Did you get all settled in?"

Dougie replied, "I did, and thank you very much. It's a really nice place, very pastoral. Molly checked me in, and she was kind enough to even make some tea for me."

"My wife, Wilma Jean, must be out flying," Bud replied.

"Flying?"

"She has what you might call a bush plane business. Supplies folks in the backcountry."

"Seems like there's a lot in common between where we both live —bush planes, remote backcountry, eccentric people..."

"Eccentric people?" Bud asked.

"That woman who just called. She reminds me of stuff we deal with all the time."

"Oh, Mrs. Jensen." Bud replied. "She's pretty elderly, gets confused easily. But sometimes this place does remind me of an outdoors asylum, but generally in a good way."

"Do you know a fellow named Jacob Doyle? Would you say that about him?"

Dougie's tone had changed, and Bud immediately had the feeling he was walking into something he might not necessarily want to walk into.

"Jacob Doyle? No, I've never heard the name. He's from Green River?"

"Yes, according to what we can find about him."

"Did he do something up North?" Bud asked.

"He did, at least he's the prime suspect, but always innocent until proven guilty," Dougie replied.

"What exactly did he do?"

Dougie replied, "Doyle's a rather prominent geologist, came into our country some time ago for research and had a good reputation until...well he's suspected of murdering one of his fellow geologists— not a very kind thing to do to one in your own profession, I would add, or to anyone, for that matter. And you're sure you don't know him? Someone world renowned from your own small town?" Dougie now sounded skeptical.

Bud replied measuredly, "I'm sure. I've never heard of him." He was beginning to get the distinct feeling that RCMP Officer Dougald McDougald didn't believe him.

"Well, Sheriff Shumway, I have evidence that he knows you, in spite of what you're saying, and that you may know exactly where he is. I think it would behoove you to cooperate with us, especially since our two countries have an interagency agreement for such. We want to find this man—we *will* find this man—and bring him to justice."

Dougie now stood and opened the door, then turned back to Bud, saying, "I have a few others on my list to talk to, then I'll be back. You know, Doyle can try to hide, but there'll be a slip-up, there always is. We know he's still in Yukon Territory, and if you can convince him to give himself up, he'll have plenty of chance for a fair trial. But then again, if he doesn't come in, bones scattered by wolves and bears in the bush don't get *any* kind of trial. The Yukon can be a cold and inhospitable place, and our Canadian wilderness can deliver a special form of justice."

With that, he walked out the door, leaving a distinct wake of discontent, making Bud wish he'd skipped that morning cup of coffee at the cafe and instead gone on out with the dogs.

3

Try as he might, Bud couldn't recall ever having met anyone named Jacob Doyle.

He tried calling Wilma Jean, but she was apparently out of range, as he couldn't get anything but her voice mail.

He wasn't used to having someone treat him as if he was lying, and it didn't set well. Whoever this Dougie McDougald fellow was, Bud felt he lacked somewhat in the diplomacy department, and even though it bothered him, he knew there was nothing the RCMP could do to him without evidence. And he sure couldn't change his mind and suddenly know something he didn't already know.

Or maybe he could, he mused, now remembering the envelope in his desk drawer. Did it hold some kind of information that the Mounties thought he already knew, and which he would then know after he opened it?

He put the envelope back into the drawer. If he didn't open it, he would be innocent in the event it did hold incriminating information, Bud thought.

On the other hand, if it did, why not just take it to Dougie and show him and be done with the whole matter? Or was he somehow being set up, though why anyone would have a motive to do such a thing was beyond him.

Bud shook his head, amazed at how quickly one's mind could get discombobulated. He'd done nothing wrong, and he wasn't going to let anyone make him worry that he had. After all, he mused, fear was the most effective tool in the arsenal of those who wished to control others.

He took out his pocket knife, carefully opening the envelope, which contained one large sheet of thick paper on the official letter-head of the Dawson Mining Recorder.

To his surprise, it was a certificate saying one Jacob Doyle of Whitehorse, Yukon Territory, Canada, had legally transferred a mining claim to him, Bud Shumway, of Green River, Utah, U.S.A.

Bud carefully put the certificate back into the envelope and stuck it into the desk drawer. He then absentmindedly pulled a small harmonica from his pocket, leaned back in his chair, feet on desk, and began playing *Red River Valley*.

Bud was a consummate fiddler, doing his best thinking while fiddling with something, his latest device being a harmonica he'd found over in the grade-school yard.

He'd pretty much mastered *Red River Valley* and was ready to move onto something new, maybe something like that old Johnny Horton tune, *North to Alaska*. He tried humming it for a moment, then, deciding it was too complicated for beginner harmonica, moved on to something a bit more regional, *Ghost Riders in the Sky*.

He was doing pretty well, he thought, especially for such a rank beginner, until things kind of began to fall apart as he got to the *yippie kiy-oh, yippie kiy-ay* part.

It was then that he put his feet down from his desk and put the harmonica back in his pocket, suddenly standing up. That was it! He'd figured out who Jacob Doyle was! If it was a snake it would've bit him!

Jacob Doyle was none other than Shorty Doyle, his old high-school science teacher. It had taken awhile for his subconscious to register it, because nobody ever referred to Shorty as Jacob. The only reason he even remembered it at all was because Shorty had always signed Bud's report card as Jacob Doyle, but to everyone in Green River, he was Shorty.

Bud sat back down, again pulling out his harmonica, going back to his old standby, *Red River Valley*.

When had Shorty Doyle gone to Canada? Bud tried to think back. Shorty had been one of Bud's younger teachers, fresh out of college, and everyone in town had seemed to think highly of him. Bud really couldn't remember much about him, except he was an amiable fellow, tall and gangly, and easy-going with a unique talent for making science fun and understandable.

Bud could still remember some of the science experiments they'd done in class, especially the one where they'd built a replica of Vesuvius, which included drowning the miniature town of Pompeii in somewhat greasy ashes collected from Shorty's barbecue.

He vaguely recalled something about Shorty going back to college to get a graduate degree in something or other. Shorty's parents were from Green River, and he'd grown up here, but he'd apparently gone on to other things after getting his graduate degree, which must have included some kind of research up North. Shorty's parents had both passed away and were long gone.

Again putting the harmonica back in his pocket, Bud took the Green River phone book from his desk drawer. He knew if anyone in Green River was likely to know anything about Shorty, it would be Cassie Rose, Green River's current high-school science teacher.

"Cassie speaking," answered a soft voice that reminded Bud of flowing water. Maybe he should go on out to the irrigation ditch on the farm and play stick with the dogs, Bud thought, then remembered he'd shut off the water after the harvest.

"Cassie, this is Bud Shumway. Am I calling at a good time?"

"Of course, Bud. I'm just getting ready to make some lunch for me and Whiskerbiscuit."

"Whiskerbiscuit?"

Cassie laughed. "My cat. She's kind of white with brown on the edges, chubby, like a biscuit with whiskers."

"Oh, sure, sure," Bud replied. "Cassie, I'm trying to figure out what ever became of my old high-school science teacher, Shorty Doyle, also known as Jacob Doyle. Do you have any idea?"

"Gosh, Bud, that would be a really long time ago, way before my time," Cassie teased.

Bud laughed. "Only a good 30 years or so. Jeez Louise, can that be? Thirty years since I was in high school? Where did the time go?"

"Well, that we should all age as gracefully as you, Bud. But actually, I do know what happened to Shorty. He got a graduate degree in geology from Stanford and taught there for awhile, then went up into Canada, where he worked for the Yukon Geological Survey. His mom was Canadian, so he has dual citizenship."

"I didn't know that," Bud replied. "And his mom ended up right here in Green River." He thought of Dougie and his comment about the similarities between the Yukon and Green River. He'd thought it was a bit far-fetched, but maybe not so much after all.

"I know all this only because he was my graduate advisor when I went to Stanford," Cassie added.

"You have a graduate degree?"

"I do, a Master's in Geology, just like Shorty, though he also has a PhD. We stayed in touch for a few years, and he tried to get me to come up there and go to work for him, but I wanted to teach, and I met my future husband, who had the ranch here, and you know the rest of the story."

Bud did indeed know the rest of the story, which unfortunately included a bad farm accident that had killed Cassie's husband, though she still had the ranch.

Cassie continued. "But Shorty became quite the celebrity up there. Canada really values their scientists and supports them. He did lots of research in the Northwest Territories and became the world expert on Hadean rocks."

"What's that?" Bud asked.

"The oldest rocks on Earth. Shorty's the one who discovered the oldest known crustal fragment, which is in the Acasta Gneiss north of Yellowknife and dated at up to 4.03 billion years old, which is pushing right up to the Earth's formation at 4.58 billion years. He hosted a science documentary for several years on CBC, the Canadian network, and became quite well known. But we were both pretty busy and eventually lost touch with each other. He's probably retired by now. I would love to see him again."

"Me, too," Bud replied. "But do you know if he was ever involved in any kind of gold prospecting?"

"Knowing Shorty, he probably was. If it had anything to do with geology, he was involved. But do you have any idea where he's at now?"

Bud sighed. "I don't, maybe still in the Yukon, but if I hear anything, I'll let you know. Thanks for the background info, and be sure and stop by the cafe next time you see my old Toyota FJ there. I'll buy you lunch."

"That would be great," Cassie said. "Tell Howie I said hello."

Bud now locked up the office, got into his FJ, and headed out to the bungalow to get the dogs. Maybe he could salvage what was left of the day, taking them out to the old missile base for a walk and a few photos, as it was too late to go to Hondu Country or Bruin Point.

But his peace of mind was gone, and why in hellsbells would a Canadian Mountie think Bud had anything to do with a man he hadn't seen for thirty-odd years, and why would that same man, a suspected murderer, sign a mineral claim in the Yukon over to him? How did he even know Bud was sheriff to have the certificate sent to his office?

Bud again fiddled with the harmonica, trying to master the *yippie kiy-oh, yippie kiy-ay* part as he drove out Long Street to King's Lane, then, barely making the turn, put it back into his pocket and drove with both hands.

As much as it pained him, he knew he had no choice. He would just have to wait and see how things panned out.

4

Bud sat in his office across from Cassie Rose, who had called him wanting to meet, even though it was long after dark. Bud had finally managed to take the dogs out for a walk and had just taken them home when she'd called.

Cassie said, "You know me, Bud, I'm a scientist. As soon as the phone went dead, I grabbed a piece of paper and wrote it all down, verbatim."

Cassie handed Bud a piece of paper. "Here's the transcription of our conversation, short and not-so-sweet."

Shorty: Cassie, you remember me—Jacob Doyle, you know, Shorty? Your grad school advisor?

Me: Of course. This is really strange. Bud Shumway and I were just talking about you. You remember Bud?

S: I do, and it's not really all that strange, as you'll find out when you talk to him again. Cassie, I only have a few minutes, there may be people listening in. I don't want to get you involved in this, but I can't get ahold of Bud.

Me: He's the sheriff, just dial the sheriff's office. I can get you the number. Hold on...

S: No, no, it's not like that. I'm trying to steer clear of direct communication with him, as they'll think he's involved. Look, I'm running out of time. You have to get a message to him, and don't let anyone know or hear what I'm about to say. Tell Bud he has to come up to the Yukon and help me out. My life depends on it. Time's running out. Cassie, you guys are my only hope now. Please, tell Bud to come right away. Tell him I'll make it worth his time.

Me: What's going on, Shorty?

S: I'm being accused of murder. I can't talk any longer. Tell him to come to the Klondike Cafe.

"And then he just hung up," Cassie said. "Bud, what's going on?"

Bud replied, "Cassie, I don't think you want to get involved in this. I'm not sure what's going on myself, but there's a Canadian Mountie in town trying to get me to confess to something I didn't do, and Shorty's involved."

"What didn't you do?"

"I don't know."

"How can you confess to something you don't even know you didn't do?"

"I'm trying to figure that one out. They're accusing him of murder. Then today, from nowhere, I got this." Bud pulled the envelope from the drawer and handed it to Cassie.

Cassie opened the envelope and studied it, then said, "He gave you a gold mining claim?"

"I sure didn't pay for it. I didn't even ask for it. In fact, I didn't even know it existed."

"And this all happened today? The Mountie visited you, claiming you know something you don't, you called me to see if I knew anything about Shorty, then you got this, and Shorty called me? Did you tell him to call me?"

"No," Bud replied. "I haven't talked to him for thirty some years, like I said when we talked earlier. The RCMP is claiming I know where he is and have contact with him."

"It almost seems like what they're claiming about you being in touch with him is coming true, doesn't it?"

"Do you think I'm being set up somehow? Do you think Shorty's really in trouble? Would I be crazy to go to the Yukon?" Bud asked.

Cassie looked thoughtful, then said, "Probably."

"And where in hellsbells is the Klondike Cafe?"

"I've never heard of it," she replied quietly, then added, "But my guess would be somewhere in the Klondike area of the Yukon. But Bud, something weird's going on here. Let's analyze it, though it's actually pretty simple. Two choices: either you're being setup to go to the Yukon for some strange reason and the Mounties are in on it, or Shorty's really in trouble and needs our help. I vote for the latter. Occam's Razor—the simplest solution is usually the correct one."

"I could see him calling you," Bud said. "But why me? I'm surprised he even remembers who I am."

Cassie smiled knowingly. "Oh, he remembers you alright. He told me all about your escapade and how you were sent from Price to Green River to straighten out or go to reform school. I was supposed to keep mum about it."

Bud groaned. "I was sixteen years old. I had the sense of an inbred squirrel. My parents sent me to stay with my Aunt Rhoda and Uncle Chet here in town until the smoke cleared. Otherwise, I would've never known Shorty, as I would've gone to Price High School that year. That's where I graduated, you know."

"Well, I found it kind of funny, to be honest. But Shorty told me he'd been contacted by your dad and asked to keep an eye on you."

"He probably asked all the teachers to do that. But did Shorty talk to you about this when you were at Stanford?"

"No, we talked about it right after you were elected sheriff. I was here and Shorty was in the Yukon, and he called me and we just got to talking about things. He was still trying to talk me into going to work up there. We just thought it was funny, that's all, for the newly elected sheriff to have, as a kid, helped steal a truck with a full load of cow manure, accidentally dumping it on the lawn at City Hall. It *was* an accident, right?"

"Not really," Bud grinned. "But it sure wasn't my idea. I just went along for the ride. Jimmy Tallman was driving. It taught me not to go along on rides, and this is starting to kind of feel like it could be one."

"Well, the upshot is that Shorty remembered you, and he knows you're the sheriff. So he probably figures you're the most likely to have the knowhow to help him. I think you should go. Do you have a passport?"

"I do, but only because Wilma Jean made me get one, thinking maybe we could go to Hawaii."

"You don't need a passport to go to Hawaii."

"I know, but she was hoping to go on to Australia from there. But we're just both too busy, and it's too expensive."

Cassie now looked thoughtful. "Bud, I'll buy you a ticket to White-horse. It'll be my way of helping out."

"You can afford that?"

"I can. I got a big settlement from my husband's death. In fact, I can help with your other expenses, too. And knowing Shorty, he'll insist on paying us back anyway. I'm very fond of him. He helped me a lot in school."

"Assuming I can help him," Bud added. "Which could be a big assumption."

"Given your reputation, Bud, I have every confidence in you. Go talk to Wilma Jean. Pack your stuff—go light, but be sure to take your camera gear. The Yukon's supposed to be a beautiful place. I'll go home and find you a ticket online and book it."

Bud looked shocked.

"But what about the boys..."

"They'll be fine without you for a week or two. I can always stop by and take them out for a walk or check on them or whatever, if Wilma Jean's busy. Howie can cover for you at the office. Nothing ever happens around here anyway."

"I'll have to talk to the mayor..."

"Rich is a good friend of mine, and I know he'll be fine after we explain everything. Look, we need to get the ball rolling. If I didn't have to teach, I'd go with you. You need to go find Shorty and the Klondike Cafe."

"The Klondike Cafe..." Bud's voice trailed off.

"You can do this, Bud. Howie and I will be command central and give you telephone support. You can call us when you need research done or stuff like that. And don't forget, it's late autumn up there, maybe even the start of winter. Take warm clothes, and now that the days are getting shorter, you'll be able to see the Aurora Borealis, the Northern Lights. Think of the photographic opportunities."

Bud's eyes lit up. "You're right!"

He stood, saying, "I'm going home right now to talk to Wilma Jean and get packed."

They both left the office, but as soon as Bud saw Cassie's taillights heading back out to her ranch, he felt a sinking feeling. He really had no desire to go anywhere, yet alone someplace as remote as the Yukon. He was pretty happy where he was.

And what if Shorty was guilty? They were assuming he wasn't, based on what they knew of him, but Bud knew people could change.

And how had Bud managed to get on the wrong side of the RCMP so quickly? They should be on the same side, he thought, as they were all just trying to keep the same law and order.

He drove slowly back to the bungalow, pulled into the drive next to his wife's big pink Mary Kay Lincoln Continental, then got out and went into the back yard, sitting in one of the wicker chairs under the big globe willow in the dark.

The kitchen light was on, and he knew Wilma Jean was probably wondering where he was. He needed to go inside and let her know what was going on.

Instead, he felt a strange poignancy, a feeling that he was leaving the place he loved best and might never return.

As he sat, he quietly began singing.

> From this valley they say you are leaving,
> We will miss your bright eyes and sweet smile.
> For they say you are taking the sunshine,

That has brightened our pathways awhile.
Come and sit by my side if you love me,
Do not hasten to bid me adieu.
But remember the Red River Valley,
And the cowboy who loves you so true.

He finally stood and quietly walked into the house.

5

Bud sat in the concourse at the Salt Lake City Airport, feeling about as out of place as he had when he'd stood in front of the judge over the manure truck incident when he was sixteen.

Actually, at this point in time, he figured he would actually prefer the judge to the restless crowd that surrounded him, all in a hurry to get to who knows where, though he did know that they were on their way to Seattle along with him, according to the concourse display.

Just then, his phone rang.

"Yell-ow," he answered, seeing from the caller ID that it was Wilma Jean.

"Hon, where are you?"

"The plane's been delayed. Still in Salt Lake."

"That's too bad. I'm at the cafe, and there was a guy in here asking for you. I told him you were leaving the country. It was supposed to be a little joke, but he seemed to take it very seriously. He wanted to know why you had flown the coop without telling him."

Bud groaned. "Was his name Dougie McDougald?"

"How did you know?"

Bud replied, "Just a hunch. And was he wanting you to make him poutine?"

"What's poutine? No, he wanted something called Timbits. When I finally figured out what he was talking about, I sent him over to the Chow Down, telling him we don't do donuts, yet alone donut holes."

"It's a Tim Horton's thing," Bud replied. "Kind of a Canadian Star-buck's. Did you tell him exactly where I was going?"

"I just said Canada. He sure seemed put out."

"He's that Mountie I told you about," Bud said.

"Oh no! I probably shouldn't have said anything!"

"He'll figure it out anyway. He's the one who stayed at the Melon View."

"That guy? Molly said he was a great guest. He invited her and Kale to visit him up North. They got to be good friends."

"He's probably not all bad," Bud replied.

Wilma Jean said, "Well, let me know when you get there. We already miss you."

Bud sighed. He hadn't even left Utah yet, and he was ready to go home.

"Maybe you could bring the boys and fly up to Whitehorse."

"Now that's a thought," she replied.

Bud felt a surge of hope. "Really?"

"Hon, you just get done what you need to do and come home. Take lots of pictures."

She was gone, and Bud suddenly felt deflated and alone. That was soon replaced by a sense of disappointment in himself. Here he was, on his way to high adventure in one of the places he'd always wanted to visit ever since reading books like *The Call of the Wild*, and he was already as homesick as a little kid leaving his family for summer church camp.

He pulled out his harmonica, then decided it would be too intrusive to play it, putting it back in his pocket.

He'd caused quite a stir when going through the airport metal detector, having forgotten it was in his pocket. A rather large and intimidating security guard had pulled him aside, and he'd actually had to play a few bars to convince him it was indeed a working harmonica and not some devious disguised bomb-like device.

It had been Bud's first audience, not counting his wife and the dogs, and several people had stopped to listen to him again try to conquer the *yippie kiy-oh, yippie kiy-ay* part of *Ghost Riders in the Sky*. He'd stopped in embarrassment when people started clapping. But even at that, he'd felt proud to have tried and given it his best.

He was now beginning to wonder if they would ever board the plane when his phone rang again. He could see it was Howie.

"Yell-ow," he answered.

"Sheriff! Are you in the air yet?" Howie sounded excited. "The mayor just told me you're going to be gone for a week or two. I can cover for you, though things at the drive-in are starting to heat up. I had three people stop by yesterday wanting BBQ sandwiches when they saw me inside cleaning. So, you're going up to the land of the Midnight Sun, up to Robert Frost country?"

Bud laughed. "Well, I think Robert Frost was back East, if I recall. Maybe you mean Robert Service."

"*The Call of the Wild*," Howie replied.

"No, that was Jack London. But Howie, they're starting to board, so I have to go."

They said goodbye, and Bud stood, hoisting his carry-on bag over his shoulder. He now felt a knot starting to grow in his stomach, that same knot that always came around to join in when his dislike of flying reared its head.

He hadn't flown in a commercial jet for a long time—in fact, he wasn't sure he ever had—and even though he'd flown a time or two in his wife's small plane, he wasn't looking forward to the flight. Maybe he could just go to sleep and not wake up until the plane landed, even though he'd asked for a window seat so he could maybe take photos. He'd been surprised to see he was flying with Alaska Airlines, as he didn't think they came as far south as Salt Lake.

Bud found his seat, tucking his bag up under his feet, not wanting to put it in the overhead compartment, cautious because it held his camera gear, as well as the gold mining claim.

Soon, an older woman in a long skirt, boots, and tweed jacket sat next to him, and he nodded his head congenially, then turned to the action out his window as the loading gate backed away from the plane. He knew they would soon be taking off, though he tried not to think about it, fiddling with the harmonica in his shirt pocket, fighting the compulsion to take it out.

Finally, he turned to the woman, and wanting to take his mind off things, asked, "You going to Seattle?"

"I think we all are," she smiled.

Bud smiled back, feeling a bit deflated. The woman, as if sensing his discomfort, added, "And then on to Whitehorse."

Bud, now encouraged, said, "Whitehorse? Me, too. My first time there. Do you live there?"

"No," she replied. "I live in Dawson City, if you know where that is, but I spend a lot of time in Whitehorse."

"Dawson City—headquarters of the Klondike Gold Rush," Bud replied, having done an Internet search the previous night.

She seemed pleased. "You'd be surprised at how many have never heard of it."

"Only around 2,000 people there, but you get a lot of tourists, right?" Bud was eager to make small talk, as the plane was now moving away from the concourse.

"We do. It looks like you're a photographer."

She pointed to his bag on the floor.

Bud had decided before he left that going north to take photos of the Aurora Borealis would be a good cover story.

"I've always wanted to film the aurora," he said. "Now I finally get to."

"Are you a professional?" she asked.

"No, I'm a melon farmer," Bud replied, which, though true, wasn't the whole story, but he wasn't sure anyone needed to know he was also a sheriff.

"And you?" He asked, thinking she was probably retired.

"I'm with the RCMP," she replied, smiling. "You know, the Mounties. Surely you've heard of us?"

Bud groaned silently, then said, "Yes, you always get your man." He then turned to the view out the window.

Perhaps he hadn't given Dougie the slip after all.

6

Bud would never forget the words of his grandfather when he'd been younger. They were cowboying on the Preston Nutter Ranch, up in Nine Mile Canyon out of Price.

Bud was a young lad, spending the summer helping his grandfather, who managed the place. They'd stopped to talk with an old grizzled cowpuncher who was riding across one of the Nutter pastures, heading north up towards the Ute reservation.

After making small talk, the cowboy had moved along, and Bud had then asked his grandpa why he hadn't asked him his name or where he was going.

"Buddy, it's the unspoken Code of the West to never ask. You don't know who you're talking to, and it's none of your business. And quite often you're better off not knowing."

Bud was glad he hadn't told the woman next to him much about himself, and he had no intentions of asking her any questions at all, thinking back to what his grandpa had said.

But he had the feeling that she already knew more about him than he would have liked. For him to board a plane for Whitehorse to go looking for Shorty Doyle and have someone with the RCMP sit next to him was just too big of a coincidence. He would now be her captive audience all the way to Whitehorse, and he'd have to be careful what he said and not slip up, for surely she was part of Dougie's team.

But how had they known he'd be on the plane? They must've somehow listened in on his conversation with Cassie. Had they somehow bugged his office? It would be totally illegal without a judge's order, and Bud knew Judge Richter at the county seat over in Castle Dale wouldn't be very amenable to something like that, especially given Bud's sterling reputation as county sheriff. Besides, the RCMP had no jurisdiction to even ask something like that.

And hadn't Wilma Jean said Dougie was put out upon finding Bud had left? Why would he be upset if he'd already known? And how had they managed to get a seat next to him on a full plane, especially when Cassie had booked his at the last minute? Could it all be just a coincidence? If so, Bud figured he'd used up his strange coincidences quota for the next decade or two.

The plane was now taking off, and Bud could no longer resist the urge to fiddle with something, so he took the harmonica out, running his fingers across it with his eyes closed.

The sound of the engines drowned everything out, and he could feel the force of the sudden speed pushing him back. He suddenly wanted nothing more than to be sitting on a tractor back at the farm, or even trying to convince Old Man Green that it's illegal to sell hard watermelon spritzer without a liquor license. And he swore that if he made it through all this alive he would never again get impatient with Howie's endless questions.

The plane gradually leveled out, and Bud put the harmonica back in his pocket, now looking out the window. They were already out over the Great Salt Lake, and he could see the freeway in the distance, the cars looking like miniature toys.

His ears popped a bit, and he tried to relax, leaning back in his seat, glancing at the woman next to him, who was now flipping through the in-flight magazine. For someone tracking him, she sure didn't seem very interested in talking, he noted.

He closed his eyes, and before he knew it, the flight attendant's voice was waking him, telling everyone they would soon be landing in Seattle. Looking out the window, he could see the giant volcanic shape of Mt. Rainier, its top hidden in clouds.

He was glad he'd slept through the flight, figuring it must've been his defense mechanism for the stress. Surprised by how quickly they landed, he leaned back, happy to be back on the ground, relieved.

He watched as everyone got off, including the woman next to him. He figured she must have gone to get a coffee or snack in the concourse and wondered how long the layover here at the Sea-Tac airport would be as he again closed his eyes.

When he awoke, he found himself slipped down in his seat, alone on the plane. It appeared that he was the only one continuing on to Whitehorse, he mused, finding it somewhat odd. How could they afford to run a flight with only one passenger? And where was the RCMP woman? Probably still in the concourse or maybe the washroom, he figured, which would make two passengers, still pretty slim pickings.

Since the plane was empty, he again pulled out his harmonica, this time trying something new—*The Tennessee Waltz*. He was getting it going pretty good when several people came on board with cleaning supplies, whisking through the plane in a flash, smiling at Bud and encouraging him to continue playing as they cleaned.

"Nice of them to clean things up a bit," he thought, as the main door again opened and several flight attendants came on board, checking through supplies and such, none paying him any mind.

Before long, the plane began filling with new passengers, which relieved Bud, as he was beginning to wonder what was going on and if they would ever get back in the air.

A youngish tanned guy who looked like an outdoors type sat next to him, and Bud nodded congenially, then again looked out the window. The ramp was now pulling away, and he knew they would soon be taking off, as the flight attendant had told everyone to buckle up.

Bud felt a little better this time, now having gone though all this before, though he wondered why the RCMP woman had decided not to sit by him. Oh well, it was for the best, he decided, as that way he wouldn't accidentally tell her anything he might regret later.

The plane soon lifted off, but this time Bud kept his eyes open, looking out the window. He was amazed at how quickly they gained altitude.

But he was even more amazed when the flight attendant came on and said, "Welcome to Alaska Airlines. We should arrive in Anchorage in approximately two hours. Thank you for flying with us."

7

Bud was pretty sure that Anchorage wasn't on the way to Whitehorse, but turning to the young guy next to him, he asked, "Looks like we're taking the long way to Whitehorse, eh?"

"Whitehorse? You mean in the Yukon? No, I don't think this plane goes to Whitehorse. Is that where you're trying to go?"

Bud replied, embarrassed, "I think I was supposed to switch planes back there. I'm not what you'd call a frequent flyer. In fact, I'm not even an infrequent flyer."

The young guy laughed. "And nobody noticed? It's pretty hard to not get kicked off after they land unless it's a through flight."

"I went to sleep and was kind of slumped down."

"Well, I'm pretty sure you can get a flight from Anchorage to Whitehorse. I don't know. You might have to go through Fairbanks first."

"Do you think they'll honor my ticket, seeing how it was my fault?" Bud was keenly aware of how little money he had.

"Not so sure about that," the guy said. "But my name's Curt Seagrove. My family lives in Anchorage."

"Bud Shumway," Bud replied. "I'm from Green River, Utah."

"Green River? Not *the* Green River," Curt said.

Bud wasn't sure what he meant. "Well," he replied, "I guess there's one in Wyoming, too."

Curt laughed good-naturedly. "I'm a climber when I'm not working. Some of the world's greatest desert towers are down near you—the Titan, Priest and Nuns, Airport Tower, Castle Rock, not to mention Indian Creek. I've stopped in your little town many times to resupply."

"Next time, don't be a stranger," Bud kidded. "But seriously, my wife and I own a farm there, and she runs a cafe and B&B. We'd be glad to have you stop in."

"I'll probably take you up on that, though I won't be back down that way until next spring. I'm a doctor at the clinic in Skagway and have to plan my time off pretty carefully."

"Where's Skagway?" Bud asked. "Isn't that where all the bears are?"

"Well, we do have bears, but I bet you're thinking of Hyder, as that's where they have the viewing platforms for the salmon run. Skagway is right on the Alaska-Canada border, south of Whitehorse. It gets a lot of tourists—the big cruise ships. It's part of the Klondike Gold Rush history."

Bud suddenly wished he could disappear, and Hyder sounded about right. Maybe he could go feral, catch salmon with the bears and forget about how incompetent he was as an adventurer. So far, he'd totally botched getting to Whitehorse, and who knew what would come next? He was suddenly homesick again, wondering what the dogs were doing.

Curt continued. "Hey, I have a thought! My uncle has a float plane. He's flying me to Skagway tomorrow. I can ask him if he has room for another passenger. You could go with me, which would put you close to Whitehorse. Everyone in Skagway goes up there for supplies and such, so you could probably easily hitch a ride and save a plane ticket. Whitehorse is only a little over a hundred miles from Skagway."

Bud wasn't sure what to think. "Is the float plane expensive?"

"I'm sure he wouldn't charge you anything, since he's already taking me. It would be a once-in-a-lifetime flight for you. Beautiful country. Did you have any bags checked?"

Bud groaned. He'd forgotten all about the one bag with his clothes and a few essentials like his toothbrush, though he hadn't packed much.

Curt said, "Not to worry. Your bag went on without you, and you can get it at the Whitehorse airport. You know, the Yukon is pretty famous for adventure, and it sounds to me like you're having one just getting there. My folks are retired teachers in Anchorage, and I'm sure they would be happy to let you stay in their guest room. I can sleep on the couch. I'll call them right now."

Bud was shocked. You could call people when on a commercial airplane thousands of feet above the ground? How did you connect with cell towers when you were going over 500 mph?

Curt talked with someone for a moment, then hung up. "My mom says you're more than welcome."

"That's really nice of you guys," Bud replied. "But say, is there something special you do to call out like that? I'd like to call my wife."

Curt grinned. "Just dial the number. They don't like you using your cell phone when they're landing or taking off, but other than that, it's OK."

Bud dialed Wilma Jean's number.

"Hon, where are you?" She answered.

"I'm on my way to Whitehorse, but I'm taking the scenic route. I won't get there until tomorrow or maybe the next day. Could you let Cassie know? I think she reserved a car for me at the airport. Could you have her cancel it? I'll rent one when I get there."

"What in the world! You might be a couple of days late? Just where are you exactly?"

Now mindful of how the Mounties seemed to know what he was doing, Bud replied, "I really can't say. But I'm fine. I'll call you tonight."

He hung up, wondering if they could trace his call. Maybe he should be more careful about calling out, use a pay phone or something, or maybe even borrow Curt's phone.

Now feeling better having this new plan for getting to Whitehorse, Bud turned to Curt and asked, "Do they have poutine in Alaska?"

Curt laughed. "Not really, that's a Canuck thing."

"Canuck?"

"Slang for Canadian. Haven't you heard of the Vancouver Canucks, the hockey team?"

"Not really. We don't play much hockey in Green River."

A flight attendant now came around, offering them snacks from a tray. Bud took a small package of peanuts, thinking of how Howie had tried to grow peanuts there on his small acreage out of Green River. He suddenly missed him.

He turned again to Curt, asking, "Have you lived up here all your life?"

"I have. All 32 years."

"And you like it up here? Don't the winters get a bit long?"

"You get used to them, especially if you've never known anything else. When you go to the Lower 48, you'll find it kind of haunts you when you're gone. It's hard to forget the North."

Bud smiled, thinking how he would never forget this trip, for sure.

Curt continued. "I've spent a lot of time in your desert, and it's much the same way. There's something about both places that you can't find anywhere else, a kind of richness of feeling. And up here, you can almost live a life...well you can still live the way we were designed to live, close to nature."

"I think you're right. I definitely feel that way about the desert," Bud said.

"Be careful," Curt warned. "The North gets under your skin. You can never forget it—it comes back to haunt you at the most unlikely times. But look, there's Turnagain Arm. We're almost in Anchorage. I'd really enjoy showing you around some if you're not too tired—we can drive north a ways and see if Denali's showing its face."

Bud grinned. It appeared that his luck had changed, and maybe things would turn out OK after all.

Shorty Doyle and the Klondike Cafe were all but forgotten for the time being.

8

Bud couldn't believe how lucky he was, as he sat looking out the window of the railroad car as the train passed through a long valley surrounded by forbidding glacial-scrubbed mountains. In fact, he not only felt lucky, but couldn't believe how quickly things had changed for the better since he'd met Curt on the plane to Anchorage.

Some people were just like that, he mused, generous and caring and making the lives of those around them better. He resolved to be more like that in the future.

Curt had gone out of his way to show Bud around, and they'd even been able to see Denali in the far distance after driving up near Wasilla. If Curt ever came to Green River, which Bud was sure he would, he knew he and Wilma Jean would do everything they could to make his visit the best ever.

Bud was now the only passenger on the White Pass and Yukon Narrow Gauge Railroad, which technically had shut down for the tourist season but would pick up a large group of hikers who had hiked the Chilkoot Pass Trail to Bennett Lake.

The hikers had contracted a special charter with the train and would be returning to Skagway, but Bud would get off at the little town of Carcross, where Curt was sure he could catch a ride to Whitehorse, which would only be around 50 miles away at that point.

Curt had somehow managed to get a Bud a free pass, saying something about knowing everyone in Skagway because he was a doctor. The ride had been impressive, cutting through the massive Coast Mountains through two long tunnels and over sky-high trestles near cascading waterfalls, until they'd finally summited White Pass, then they'd dropped back down and passed though the small town of Fraser.

Now the conductor, the only other one on the train other than the engineer, entered the car and sat down across from Bud.

"Welcome to Canada," he said.

"Canada?" Bud replied. "We're in Canada?"

"We're in British Columbia, and the Yukon is about halfway up Bennett Lake, that blue you see in the distance. We're right at the corner where the two come together with Alaska."

"This sure is beautiful country," Bud replied. "But it's a bit intimidating. You'd have to be pretty hardy to survive on your own out here."

The conductor replied, "Can you imagine being a gold prospector, they called them Stampeders, coming up here and leaving your family, trying to haul a ton of supplies over Chilkoot Pass on up to Dawson City? A lot of them didn't make it."

"A ton of supplies?"

"Yes, the Canadian Government got tired of burying dead prospectors, so they made it mandatory that you bring a year's worth of food and supplies. All in all, what they required weighed about a ton. The Klondike Gold Rush brought over 100,000 people into this area. It actually changed the entire population dynamics of not only the Yukon, but also parts of British Columbia and even Seattle. This railroad you're on was actually built to haul supplies in and gold out. It was the biggest gold rush in history. Our little town of Skagway gets over a million visitors a year, all coming to check out the lore of the Klondike. But in reality, it was a harsh rough business."

"If we're in Canada, why didn't we go through customs?" Bud asked.

"The border station's at Fraser, and it depends on where we stop as to whether you need a passport or not. Just to come to the south end of Bennett Lake doesn't require one, since we turn around after picking up people on their way back to Skagway from hiking the pass."

"Where will I go through customs?" Bud asked with concern. The last thing he wanted to do was enter Canada illegally.

The conductor now looked thoughtful. "Well, I'm not sure. I'm actually fairly new at this. You're kind of a special case," he smiled. "But you do have a passport, don't you?"

"I do," Bud replied.

"Well, if anyone asks, just show it to them and I'm sure all will be OK. Dr. Curt is a friend of mine. He delivered both of my kids. I'm more than glad to help you out, and I don't think you'll have any trouble at all. Lots of people stop in Carcross, and you should be able to easily catch a ride on up to Whitehorse."

"Carcross, that's an interesting name," Bud mused.

"It's short for Caribou Crossing."

"Interesting," Bud replied. "And we're in the Klondike now? I thought it was more up by Dawson City."

"This is all Klondike country, as it was all part of the gold rush. Skagway's the start of the South Klondike Highway, which merges with the Alaska Highway and goes through Whitehorse, then splits off north of there and turns into the North Klondike Highway and goes on up to Dawson," the conductor replied. "But Dawson City is the center of all the gold stuff."

Bud hesitated, then asked, "Have you ever heard of the Klondike Cafe?"

The conductor paused for a moment, then said, "You know, that sounds awfully familiar. I'll have to think about it, but off the top of my head, I'm not sure where it is. Do you know someone there?"

Bud, now mindful that he was maybe walking on thin ice, decided to go ahead and ask. "Do you know a guy named Jacob Doyle?"

"Jacob Doyle? Do you mean the TV science guy? I can't say I know him personally, but everyone in Canada's seen his show at one time or another. That guy?"

Bud decided it might be prudent to not let anyone know he was looking for Doyle after all, so said, "I just heard he was maybe living around here somewhere."

"Really? I think if he were, everyone would know it. He's pretty well-known. But we'll soon be to the southern shore of Bennett Lake, where you'll get off."

Bud now said with concern, "Curt said I should get off at Carcross."

"Well, that would be better, but we're not going that far, though in the summer we do. We're stopping at the station in old Bennett City, though it's closed for the season. You can just walk along the shore on the tracks and you'll eventually get to Carcross. The days are still long, and you're lucky the bugs are all gone by this time of year. Anyway, I need to get back to work, so here's to having a great time in the Yukon."

Now the train slowed, and Bud could see they were coming into a station at the edge of a large narrow lake. He could see what looked like a small crowd waiting, and as the train gradually stopped, Bud knew this was the ghost town of Bennett City, where he got off.

He grabbed his camera pack and let himself down off the steps of the railcar just as a group of about 30 weary looking hikers began boarding.

He stood watching them somewhat mournfully, wondering where all his good luck had gone. He'd thought he was getting off in Carcross, and now things seemed very uncertain, and he wasn't even sure where it actually was.

Now a woman with what he thought might be a British accent looked him up and down and then said, "Are you going to hike back down the Chilkoot? If you don't mind me saying, you don't look very well prepared. Here. I'm going home, and I won't be needing this."

With that, she took her daypack off, rummaged through it and took out a small camera, then handed the pack to Bud and quickly boarded the train before he could even thank her.

Bud looked inside. It held a small bottle of water, a red bandana, a package of Band-Aids, a small fold-up plastic jacket, a metal spoon-fork combination, a box of matches, a small can of bear spray, and what looked to be several packages of beef jerky and trail mix. It also held a small pamphlet that read:

Be prepared with our Wildness Kit, complete with titanium spork. Our special wild experts have spent many years in the Wildness preparing everything you need for safety in any enviro. Fire, bears, snakes, and even bad things as blizzards and tornadoes all covered. Buy with confidence. Made in Thailand.

Bud grinned, thinking maybe his luck had held after all, if only a little. Putting the Wildness Kit into his larger pack, he then hung the empty daypack on a tree limb. He hated to just leave it out there, but maybe someone would find it useful at some point.

Bud, now a little away from the train, took out his camera to get a photo of the last of the hikers boarding. It was all very picturesque with the yellow and green engines, and he snapped a bunch of shots, then noticed the last hiker to get on had turned away, looking irritated.

The guy seemed somewhat out of place with the rest of the group, Bud thought, as they all looked like they'd been outfitted by L.L. Bean or REI, and he looked more like someone who spent a lot of time in the bush. His jeans and flannel shirt looked well-worn, and he carried a canvas pack instead of the fancier nylon ones. The pack looked heavy, and he seemed to take some effort to swing it along with him up the train steps, and he also seemed to be limping.

He must be old school, Bud thought, or maybe he was the guide. In any case, they had all soon boarded and Bud stood and watched as the train slowly chugged away, disappearing in the distance, leaving nothing behind but a cloud of steam.

He then turned and gazed down the shore of Bennett Lake. All he could see was the rails going into a vast wilderness along the lakeshore, and he wondered if maybe his luck hadn't gone south after all.

9

The conductor had told Bud he could just walk along the shore on the tracks and soon be at Carcross, but all Bud could see was an endless glacial lake lined with towering snowcapped peaks.

He wished he'd asked the guy how far it actually was to the small town, but things had quickly gotten hectic, with the hikers boarding and all. For all Bud knew, it could be a hundred miles or more.

For a moment, he thought he might just walk the tracks back to Fraser, but he knew that was a long ways, and hopefully Carcross was much closer. Besides, getting back to Fraser meant following the rails across a barren glacial mountainside, and the lake was much more beckoning.

He began walking along the tracks, which cut between the lakeshore and thick forests of aspen and spruce that marched up the steep mountainsides, disappearing into snowfields and glaciers high above. And even though it was still early afternoon, the sun was low in the southern sky, its oblique light filtering through the trees. A chilly breeze coming from the lake reminded Bud that it was late autumn in these parts, and a big winter storm could come any time.

Bud wished he had his coat, but it was in his bag, probably sitting in the Whitehorse Airport. He was wearing a heavy flannel shirt, and he hoped it would be enough to get him to Carcross, where he could hopefully catch a ride, or even get a room if necessary.

He could see a long ways down the lake, maybe even what he guessed to be a good ten or fifteen miles, and he saw nothing that looked like a town, or even any kind of civilization, for that matter— no cabins, no roads, nothing but the silver rail stretching endlessly, following the shore.

After an hour or so of slogging along, Bud stopped for a break, taking some trail mix and the bottle of water from his pack. He'd had lunch with Curt before boarding the train back in Skagway but was already hungry again, and the fruit and nuts helped his lagging energy.

It was hard to gauge how far he'd come, but he figured it must be several miles, maybe even three or four, as he'd tried to keep up a steady pace, though it was hard walking along the rails. He was glad he was in pretty good shape from working on the farm all summer.

As he sat on a large rock, he thought of how unlikely it was for him to be there, how even as recently as this morning he would never have predicted he'd be walking a narrow-gauge line beneath immense mountains along a long deep glacial lake in British Columbia. On a whim, he took out his cell phone, but just as he'd figured, there was no service.

The scenery was stunning, unlike anything he'd ever seen, and deciding to make the best of things, he took his camera from his pack and started taking photos. For a moment, he felt a surge of happiness, for here he was, taking photos in the Canadian wilderness, something he'd always wanted to do. He hadn't really thought much about the logistics of it, though, and would never have guessed it would happen like this.

After taking a number of photos, he again sat back, thinking of his wife and the dogs, wondering what they were doing. It was probably a beautiful autumn day in the desert back home, one of the nicest times of the year, and he figured if he'd just gone on up to Bruin Point with the dogs instead of stopping for a cup of coffee at the Melon Rind, he would probably still be back in Green River, having avoided meeting up with Dougie McDougald. But given the tenacity that Mounties were known for, odds were good Dougie would've eventually found him.

He pulled the harmonica from his pocket and started making up his own song, which he knew he couldn't mess up, since nobody knew how it was supposed to go.

Now he thought of the woman on the plane, who'd said she was also a Mountie, and Bud again wondered how they'd been able to engineer getting a seat next to him on such short notice. He stopped playing the harmonica long enough to grin, for it sure looked like he'd given them the slip at this point, even though unintentionally.

He was getting sleepy, but the breeze was now becoming more of a cold wind, so Bud decided he should get going, maybe trying to make better time, for the lake didn't even appear to have changed any since he'd started, but still stretched out forever. He didn't seem any closer to anything than before.

As he stood, the sunlight lit something between the rails, and Bud bent and picked it up. It was tiny, but the sun blazed on it like a diamond! It was definitely out of place, for the rail base was some kind of dark rock that looked like it could be volcanic.

The small stone wasn't faceted like one would expect a diamond to be, Bud mused, gently biting into it, thinking maybe it was something softer, like a small piece of mica. His teeth made no dent, so he pulled out his harmonica. The stone easily scratched the metal.

He now remembered the Wildness Kit in his pack and took out the titanium spork. He wasn't positive, but he thought titanium was a very hard metal, and surely if this were some type of quartz, it would start to chip off if he tried to carve into the titanium with it.

To Bud's surprise, the small rock easily scratched the titanium, and he was beginning to think he'd found a diamond. He recalled another diamond he'd found back near Green River, and this was beginning to remind him of it, though this one was much smaller.

He took the small rock and carefully placed it inside the box of matches, about the only safe place he could think of, then put it back in his pack. He had no idea where the stone had come from, but if he were going to find diamonds while out walking the tracks, it certainly would make his time more interesting, and possibly more lucrative. Bud grinned, knowing it had to be a fluke.

Just as he was hoisting his pack back on, he thought he could hear voices on the wind, coming from the lake. He yelled "cou-eeee" several times as loud as he could, the old cowboy signal he'd learned as a lad working on the Nutter Ranch years ago in what seemed like a different world, a world of juniper trees and sagebrush and cattle, a world foreign to this land of glacial ice and imposing peaks and tall forest.

Listening carefully, he heard nothing, just the sound of the growing waves lapping on the shore. Had he heard a sound of voices long gone, of the ghosts of prospectors from the gold rush? He'd read that Bennett Lake had once been filled with thousands of rafts of gold-seekers who had stripped the forests along the lake to build boats that would take them and their tons of supplies from the top of Chilkoot Pass on to Carcross, then on down the mighty Yukon to Whitehorse and Dawson City.

Bud shivered in the wind. No matter how dire his situation became, he was better off than any of them had been, for as soon as he got to Carcross, he could rejoin civilization and not have to trudge any farther. And he knew the Klondike miners were driven by greed, a relentless taskmaster to which he paid no mind.

Bud thought back to the woman handing him the small pack, and was glad to know he now had matches and could probably make it through a cold night, given the amount of driftwood on the beaches below the tracks. But if the wind picked up, things might get a bit dicey as far as a fire went, he thought, wondering how much farther it was to Carcross.

He trudged on for a couple of more hours, not wanting to stop, for the light seemed to get thinner and less substantial, and Bud knew it was because the North country was on an arc farther from the sun's rays than he was used to.

The wind was now becoming a nuisance, making it difficult to see, as it raised the fine glacial sands from the beaches, making Bud shade his eyes from the sting. He'd gone at least another three or four miles and was getting tired when he saw what looked to be some kind of structure ahead. Could he be at the edge of Carcross?

Coming closer, he could see two buildings crammed between the railroad tracks and the high bank above the lake, the building nearest the lake sitting partly on stilts. Even though it was getting late and the buildings were now in shadows, he could tell they were old and unin-habited.

As he poked around, he felt relieved, for he knew he could easily get inside and shelter through the night from the cold wind. He knew the buildings had something to do with the train, probably built way back when it was used for its original purpose of carrying miners and their supplies to and from the Klondike. It could even be a section house, Bud thought, where rail workers could spend the night, just as he intended to do, as Carcross didn't seem to be getting any closer.

He now noticed something at his feet, and picking it up, saw that it appeared to be a torn piece from someone's jeans, part of it covered with what looked to be dried blood.

Bud knew he was far from where the geologist had been killed, but he still felt like he was looking at something that could be important.

Yet he vacillated for a moment—it was probably just an old rag someone had used to clean a fish or something—then he took off his pack and removed the bandana from its plastic and carefully put the cloth fragment inside, putting it back in his pack. He then turned his attention back to the old building, thinking he'd crawl in through a window and check things out.

But as he looked in, he quickly put himself into reverse, for looking out from the shadows inside were two large yellow eyes, eyes accompanied by a ferocious-sounding growl.

Back outside, Bud hastily took off his pack, searching for the bear spray, but he was too late, for the creature had burst through the window and was coming straight for him.

10

Bud had wondered for a moment if Wilma Jean would ever know what had become of him, seeing how the train wouldn't run again until spring, which was long enough for the wilds to easily scatter his bones.

He thought of what Dougie had said about how the Canadian wilderness sometimes delivered a special form of justice, though he wasn't sure why he would merit such, though hadn't someone once said that justice was blind?

But he soon decided he was going to live after all when the creature emerged from the shadows enough that he could see it was a medium-sized yellowish dog, which was now slowly wagging its tail. It was about as thin and scruffy looking an animal as Bud had ever seen, including numerous coyotes he'd seen in the desert, some which had been pretty scraggly.

"C'mere, boy, or are you a girl?" Bud asked, holding out his hand.

The dog was wary and slunk back into the bushes, keeping an eye on Bud, though still wagging its tail.

"You sure look hungry," Bud coaxed, now taking the beef jerky from his pack. "Want a bite of this?"

He tossed it towards the little dog, who at first thought he was throwing something at it and jumped back, but soon smelled the jerky and gobbled it down.

It didn't take long for Bud to coax the dog to come sit near him by a patch of ruby-red fireweed. He fed it the rest of the jerky, wishing he had more, but the little dog seemed content as Bud ran his hands over its coat, carefully removing burrs and matted sticks.

It almost looked like a coyote, mused Bud, yet it wasn't quite as rangy and had a shorter snout, more like a working dog. It reminded Bud a lot of an Australian dingo, and even though its coat was somewhat matted and it was thin, it seemed to be in good spirits and friendly enough, at least after its initial growl, which Bud figured was just from fear.

"What in hellsbells are you doing out here in the bush all alone?" Bud asked, thinking the little dog was probably wondering the same thing about him. "Where's your home? Did you hop the train and get kicked off like the Littlest Hobo?"

Bud thought back to the TV show, which had been kind of like the Canadian version of Lassie, which his aunt had sent him on DVD when he was younger.

Maybe there was a cabin nearby or something, Bud thought, yet the dog definitely wasn't being cared for, at least not by his standards. It seemed odd for the little dingo dog to be way out here, all alone, and Bud half expected to see someone step out of the building, or even the bush.

In fact, he was sure he'd heard someone calling, but as he listened, he decided it must be the wind. Yet the dog's ears had perked forward, so Bud thought that maybe he wasn't imagining things.

Knowing how skittish the dog was and not wanting to lose it, Bud opened his pack and took the strap from his camera, then tied it into a sort of leash. The little dog let him put it around his neck.

"You're somebody's good dog, aren't you?" Bud asked. "Come with me, and we'll find a way out of here and maybe even your home, while we're at it."

The sunlight began fading, and the wind was again picking up, and Bud knew he needed to either get inside the old building or build a fire down on the beach before it was totally dark.

Just then, he saw what looked like a piece of paper stuck in the thorns of some kind of berry bush. Bud carefully removed it—it was a Baby Ruth candy-bar wrapper. Sticking it into his pocket, he found it disturbing that there would be trash way out in this pristine wilderness.

He now decided to try the building and carefully slipped through the widow, the dog jumping through behind him. It took awhile for his eyes to adjust, but there was enough light coming in that he could see it probably wasn't any place he wanted to bed down, for the entire floor was littered with what looked like packrat debris. Some kind of animal was making itself at home here, and Bud wasn't so sure it was anything he wanted for a roommate.

He was ready to go when he noticed something wadded up in the corner of the old structure, something that looked like someone's clothing or maybe even an old blanket. And though he didn't really want to poke around in grime and dust looking at someone's trash, he felt compelled to pick it up—probably his native curiosity, he decided, that same curiosity that occasionally got him into trouble but also helped him solve crimes.

He wasn't surprised to find it was a pair of men's jeans, as he knew it was possible some hobo type had used the building for shelter and maybe left their trash, but what did surprise him when he unfolded them was seeing the pant legs had several ragged tears along the shins, and there also appeared to be some blood here and there.

Talking out the scrap of cloth he'd found, he found it fit perfectly into one of the holes. Puzzled, he first took several photos, then wrapped the jeans back up and left them where he'd found them, putting the torn piece back into the plastic bag in his pack.

Not really liking the old dusty structure, Bud now decided to give the beach a shot, as he preferred being outside where he could see what was around him. He knew he could retreat to the building if the winds got too ferocious.

He was now leading the dog down the bank when he again heard what sounded like a voice.

Bud cou-eeed again as loud as he could, then listened. There was no mistake, someone was down at the lake yelling. He began making his way as fast as he could in the dim shadows, finally arriving at the lake shore, the little dog right behind him.

There, beached just below the station house was what looked to be a fishing dory with two men standing nearby. He could hear one of them say, "He's got Lindie," just as the little dog pulled loose and ran over to the men, dragging Bud's camera strap behind it.

One of the men went down on his knees and greeted the dog, who jumped all over him, and as Bud got closer, he could see the man was trying not to cry.

The other man spoke to Bud.

"You found Joe's brother's dog. We've been out here every day looking for her. Joe just refused to give up. There were times I told him we should stop, but he knew winter was coming and if we didn't find her now, it would be too late. We've been going up and down the beach, calling. How did you find her?"

Bud shrugged his shoulders, then said, "I didn't really. I was looking in the window of that old building up there and she just jumped out."

"That's the old Pennington Station," the man replied. "Have you seen anyone else out here?"

"No," Bud replied. "Nobody."

"Where's your boat?" The man asked, looking Bud up and down.

"I'm on foot," Bud said. "You have any idea how far it is to Carcross?"

"Carcross?" The man looked incredulous. "You're walking to Carcross? Man, you have at least a good 18 or 20 miles to go."

Now Joe stood, drying his eyes, and said, "You have no idea what finding this dog means to me. My brother was out here and drowned, and his dog was lost. I was beginning to think we would never find her. I needed to find her for his sake, well, and also for hers."

The second man now said, "Do you want to ride with us? We're going to Carcross. We need to get going before the winds pick up, plus it's getting dark."

Bud felt like his luck had changed again.

"You bet," he said, following them into the boat. "Maybe I can get a room there."

"Carcross doesn't have any rooms," Joe replied. "It's a small native village with no tourist accommodations, just a general store."

Bud settled into the boat. He knew his luck had changed, but it sure didn't appear it was going to let him get comfortable.

He untangled the camera strap as Joe started the boat motor and headed down the long shadowy lake towards Carcross, the little dog called Lindie curled up by his side.

11

The boat motor droned on and on as the evening became more pronounced, Bud wondering if they would get to Carcross before dark. Joe seemed to know the lake like the back of his hand, and his partner, Dan, seemed to enjoy telling Bud about the history of the area as they motored along beneath the giant snowcapped peaks.

"Pennington Station, where you found Lindie, was a section house for railroad crews back in the late 1800s. In the winter the crew members would cut large blocks of ice from the lake and put them on a train to Skagway, where they were stored in sawdust-insulated icehouses."

Bud nodded in acknowledgement, though he was starting to get cold, as the wind had picked up even more, and talk about ice wasn't helping.

Dan continued, "Lindie was born in a cabin near Lindeman Lake, near Bennett Lake. That's where she got her name. Joe's brother, Willie, got her as a pup and was very devoted to her. She's what's called a Carolina dingo. They're the only truly wild dog in America, but are dying out because of encroachment by humans, so people down there are trying to save them and get them homes."

He continued. "The guy Willie got her from brought her parents up here, trying to find a good breed to introduce to the country besides those darn huskies. Sled dogs are good when they're in front of a sled, but they take a lot of care. The fellow with Lindie's parents wanted an all-around smart dingo-type dog, one that could take care of itself and stay out of trouble, and I guess Lindie showed she can do that."

Bud patted the dog's head, though Lindie was fast asleep.

"Lindie seems to be in good hands now," Bud said, nodding towards Joe. "Are you guys from Carcross?"

Dan replied, "We are. We're Tagish First Nations. Carcross was once a hunting and fishing camp for the Tlingit and Tagish people, but it became a supply centre during the Klondike Gold Rush. Our people practiced subsistence living—fishing, hunting, gathering berries, that kind of thing—until the gold rush and then the tourists started coming in. Joe's talking about building a motel, but I don't think the council's going to let him. Just having a boatload of tourists, and I mean that literally, is about enough for one little town, maybe too much."

Bud nodded, thinking of his little town of Green River and how it was beginning to be discovered, just like everywhere else, it seemed. He thought of the Melon View B&B and his wife's cafe and bowling alley, all which benefitted from tourism, though the bowling alley not as much. His thoughts then went to Wilma Jean—she was probably worried about him, as he'd said he'd call when he got to Carcross, but it was taking longer than he'd expected.

Bud asked Joe, "Do you have any experience running a motel? My wife has a B&B, and it can really run you ragged. She actually hired a gal to pretty much run it for her."

"Where's that at?" Joe asked, turning from the rudder.

"Down in Utah," Bud replied.

"Oh," Joe said. "I thought maybe in Skagway or something. Tourism up here is a little different, as they mostly come on the big cruise ships into Skagway and then to Carcross on the train. They spend a lot of money."

"They wouldn't even be staying in your motel if you had one, Joe," said Dan. "They go back to their ships."

Joe replied, "There would be others who might come. My mom and dad were doing pretty good with their roadhouse up by Dawson City until the government came in and told them they had to upgrade their septic system, which would've been too expensive. The government said because the river had changed course and was too close to the old tanks it was hazardous. The rivers change course all the time up here. Most of them are glacially fed and meander. But that pretty much shut them and a lot of other roadhouses down."

"Are they still living there, Joe?" Dan asked.

"Yes, and I wish they'd move back down here. It's a total dead end. I have no idea how they're even making a living. Their place is falling down around them, and they're both getting too old and stoved up to do the repairs. I've told them a dozen times they can come live with me and Helen, but they won't do it."

"Maybe they like their independence," Dan commented. "But I'd happily help move them down here for one slice of your mom's Berry Delight pie."

Joe replied, "I haven't seen them for a long time. I used to go up and see them once in awhile, talk to them, but they won't come back. They don't even have a phone. Willie lived in Dawson so would go see them all the time, but I can't get away like that, with the Vancouver folks to supply."

Joe seemed to be in a bad mood, so Bud didn't ask, but he was again wondering where the Klondike Cafe was. Now that it looked like he might actually make it to Whitehorse, his thoughts had turned again to Shorty Doyle and trying to track him down.

It was now getting dark, and Bud was amazed at how well Joe seemed to know the lake. It wasn't long until they could see lights in the far distance.

"Is that Carcross?" Bud asked.

"It is," Dan replied. "Welcome to Yukon Territory, though technically we entered it about halfway up the lake."

Neither of the men had asked Bud what he was doing out hiking the rails, trying to get to their hometown, and he knew it was the same Code of the West his grandfather had mentioned—sometimes one was better off not knowing.

Now Bud asked, "Do you guys have any idea where I could spend the night? I was hoping to be in Whitehorse by now."

Dan again gave Bud a look of incredulousness, then said, "You ever been in this country before?"

Bud knew that Dan knew the answer, but said no anyway, then added in his defense, "The conductor let me off at Bennett City. I thought they were going all the way to Carcross. He said I could walk the rails. He forgot to tell me it would take a couple of days, at the very least. He said I could hitch a ride to Whitehorse from Carcross."

"It's guys like that who end up getting people killed," Joe complained angrily. "Giving people misinformation in this country is a form of potential manslaughter, in my opinion."

"Agreed," Dan agreed. "But I bet he meant Log Cabin. Lots of people hike out the old rails to Log Cabin and catch a ride on the highway. It's not that far. I think there's a shuttle bus in the summer that stops there."

Bud now thought again of Shorty Doyle and Dougie's accusation of murder. He wanted badly to ask the two men if they'd heard of Shorty, but somehow prudence, or maybe intuition, told him not to, though he wasn't sure why.

"You can come stay at my place," Joe finally said. "It's not much, but it beats freezing to death. I'll see if my uncle's going to White-horse tomorrow, and maybe he can give you a ride. He drives truck up there. I personally wouldn't ride with the double-clutching weasel, but he'll get you there, if you don't die of fear first."

Bud thanked him, then, as the lights slowly got closer, he pulled out his harmonica and asked the two men if they would mind if he played a bit. They nodded their heads in agreement as the darkness closed in.

Bud played *The Tennessee Waltz* softly and mournfully, wishing again he was home in his snug bed with Wilma Jean by his side and the dogs at his feet.

Dan and Joe both grew quiet, listening, as the boat floated closer and closer to the lights of Carcross. They soon passed under the highway bridge and on to shore, where they tied the boat up and called it a day, Bud and Lindie following them to Joe's vehicle.

12

Bud had slept well on Joe and Helen's couch, even though the couple was up early making coffee and breakfast, waking him, though he managed to drift back off.

Lindie had slept at his feet on the couch, wanting to be as close to him as possible, and he'd awakened several times during the night and felt comforted knowing she was there.

He'd helped Helen bathe the dog the evening before, and Lindie had seemed to like the idea, though Bud suspected it was because she wanted to wash off all the memories of hard times, though he suspected he was projecting his own feelings.

He was becoming fond of her, and wanting to be sure she would be well taken care of, had asked Joe if he and Helen would keep her. He was surprised by Joe's answer.

"I wish we could, but we're gone too much. Helen works over at the general store, and I'm usually out fishing, long days. I supply a dealer in Vancouver. I know Lindie will wreck the house if we leave her here alone, because she wrecked my brother's house more than once. She has what they call sepanx. We're going to have to find her a good home."

"Sepanx?" Bud asked. "What's that?"

"I dunno, just some condition when they're afraid to be alone. I heard Helen call it sepanx."

Bud grinned. "I think that's short for separation anxiety."

Joe added, "She sure takes to you."

Bud grimaced, figuring there was no way he could take the dog back to Green River.

"I have two dogs at home," he said.

"Didn't you say you had a farm?" Helen asked. "And people fly dogs around all the time."

Joe laughed. "They fly dogs around?"

She whacked his arm in mock frustration. "You know what I mean."

Bud had told them over dinner that he had a farm back in Utah, then had given them a brief rundown of missing his plane to Whitehorse to take photos of the aurora and how he'd ended up on the tracks at Bennett Lake. He'd felt it was only polite to let his hosts know a little about who he was.

Helen had seemed amused, though Joe had taken it more seriously, saying, "I still think that conductor should be reprimanded or something. You seriously could've died out there."

Bud then called Wilma Jean, who was becoming more and more skeptical that he would ever make it to Whitehorse.

"I should get there soon," he said. "Except now that I have a dog, things may get more complicated."

He was wanting to test the waters with her before telling Joe and Helen he would take Lindie.

"That's fine, hon," she replied, and he knew she was busy and not really listening. This was a good thing, thought Bud, for he could later say he'd mentioned it to her, and by then, it would be way too late, as he'd have the dog with him. He was pretty sure his dogs, Hoppie and Pierre, would welcome a new buddy to the fold, and maybe Lindie would make things more interesting, as he knew they sometimes got bored.

He had no idea how she would figure into his quest to rescue Shorty Doyle, but the more he thought about it, the more he figured the old Chinese curse must apply to dogs—when you rescue someone, you're then obligated to take care of them. If it applied to people, he was going to quit looking for Shorty, he mused.

It wasn't long before Bud was holding on for dear life in a big Bulldog truck cab on his way to Whitehorse with Joe's Uncle Walt, Lindie by his side. Bud had asked if he could play his harmonica to take his mind off Walt's driving, and he'd gone through his entire repertoire several times, trying not to look at the road.

Once in Whitehorse, he almost had Walt drop them off at the airport so he could get his luggage, but then thought better of it, wondering if the Mounties might be there waiting for him. There was nothing in his bag he couldn't easily replace, just a few clothes, and he knew if he rented a car there they would be certain to know he'd arrived. And at this point, he was in Canada illegally, which might give them a legitimate reason to arrest him.

Instead, he asked Walt to take him downtown for supplies, as he'd decided to hitchhike on up to Dawson City, figuring having a dog along would make things easier, as people might feel sorry for the dog and stop.

They drove down the long hill into town, Bud noting that the road was called Robert Service Drive. They soon passed the SS Klondike sternwheeler banked on the wide Yukon River, which Walt told Bud had run people and freight between Whitehorse and Dawson City during the gold rush days. Bud was surprised when they got into Whitehorse, as it was bigger than he'd expected.

Walt next took him to Canadian Tire, which he told Bud was better than the nearby Wal-Mart, and Bud went inside and bought a bigger pack, filling it with a sleeping bag and pad, a small tent, a new collar and leash for Lindie, dog food, a warm coat, and a few other supplies.

He noted a number of nearby restaurants, including a Tim Horton's, so offered to buy Walt lunch, saying maybe they could go to a place that served poutine.

"Thanks, but I need to get to work," Walt replied. "Besides, I hate that stuff. I have a couple of sandwiches in my lunch box. We can share those."

Walt next took Bud out north of town where the Klondike Highway split from the Alaska Highway. Finding a wide spot, he let him out by the side of the road.

"Where exactly are you headed, anyway?" He asked.

Walt was apparently not familiar with the Code of the West, Bud mused. He decided to level with him and said, "The Klondike Cafe. Do you know where that is?"

"The Klondike Cafe? Why in heckever are you wanting to go there? It's been closed for years."

Bud wasn't sure what to say, so he just replied, "I've heard the Northern Lights are especially good there. I want to take photos."

Walt looked dubious. "Why would they be any better there than anywhere else around here?"

"You know where it is?" Bud was having trouble containing his excitement.

"Shoot, yes. My sister and her husband used to run it. Like I said, it's been closed for years."

"You mean Joe's mom and dad?" Bud asked. It was his turn to be incredulous.

"Two and the same," Walt replied. "Seriously, somebody told you the aurora's better there than anywhere else?"

"Well, not exactly better, just that I'd have a better chance of seeing it there. But can you tell me where it is?"

Walt shook his head in disbelief. "Well, now I've heard it all. I guess you really are a cheechako. The cafe's just before you get to Dawson City—you turn off on the Dempster Highway, which is the road that goes up to the Arctic, then you go about five kilometers and it's right there on the right. It sits back a bit from the road, just before the end of the pavement. The place is run down and boarded up. You won't find any room or board there, in fact, Stanley and Lily will read you the riot act if you bother them. They went from running a viable roadhouse to hating the government and people in general, so you'd be well advised to leave them alone. You can camp nearby for your photos—there's an old gravel pit on down the road where nobody will bother you but the grizzlies."

Bud tried not to show his excitement at finally learning his destination, though he had no idea how far it actually was. The route had taken a few twists and turns, and he was beginning to think he would never figure it out, but here it was, right in front of him.

He now hoisted his pack over his shoulders, having first put Lindie's new collar and leash on her.

"Joe and Helen have my contact info back in the Lower 48," he told Walt, who was now back in his truck. "If you ever get down my way, look me up."

"I might just do that," Walt replied, ready to pull out.

"Hey, Walt, just one more thing," Bud shouted over the sound of the truck engine. "What's a cheechako?"

"An ignoramus," Walt grinned as he pulled onto the highway and headed back to Whitehorse. "Tell my sis hello if you do see her. Good luck!"

Bud waved goodbye and stood by the Klondike Highway, suddenly feeling forlorn and abandoned.

13

Bud pulled out his cell phone and dialed Wilma Jean, but she didn't answer, so he left a brief message saying he loved her, was OK, and hoped to be back home soon. He figured that even if the RCMP were on his trail and could track his current location through the phone call, it didn't matter, as he hopefully wouldn't be standing there for long.

He next dialed the Emery County Sheriff's Office, but all he got was a recording saying to hang up and dial 911 if it was an emergency. Bud knew the 911 number went straight to the State Trooper's offices, and he figured Howie must either be off duty or out on call and busy.

He now took out his harmonica and began fiddling, not playing much of anything, just half-heartedly going up and down the scales.

He finally put it away and stuck out his thumb. So far, not one vehicle had passed, and he had a feeling he might be standing there for some time. He was glad he'd supplied himself for camping before leaving Whitehorse.

Like flying in a commercial airliner, Bud was pretty sure he'd never hitchhiked before, and he wondered if his luck would hold and he'd get a ride all the way to the Klondike Cafe. But first, he had to get to where the Dempster and Klondike highways met, which was a good five or six hour drive away, according to Walt.

He leaned over and patted Lindie, still not sure if he was doing the right thing by taking her, though he suspected it would all work out. She licked his hand, and he knew a special bond was already forming between them.

Looking down the highway into the early afternoon sun, Bud now wondered what the mayor and good people of Green River, Utah, would think if they saw their sheriff hitchhiking down a highway in Canada's Yukon Territory with a Carolina dingo. Add to that the facts that he'd entered the country illegally and was on the run from the Royal Canadian Mounted Police, all while on his way to help an accused murderer, and he figured that the mayor might be looking for a new sheriff. And on top of all that, Bud figured that hitchhiking was probably illegal in Canada.

He grinned at the thought of where his adventure had taken him so far—it had gone more than just distance, but had also served to reassure his faith that most people were good-hearted and would help the proverbial stranger in need.

He gave Lindie a Barkie Biscuit, fresh from Canadian Tire, then noticed a long white van coming down the highway.

The van quickly came to a screeching halt right next to him, Bud barely having time to pull Lindie aside while noting the words, "Girls on Sticks," scrawled in the dirt on its side, along with "Hockey Forever."

A woman leaned out the passenger window and asked, "Going to Dawson?"

"Just before Dawson, the Dempster Highway," Bud replied.

"That's where we're going," the woman said. "Hop in."

The van's side door slid open, and Bud hoisted his pack in and lifted Lindie inside, just as an old pickup pulled over.

Bud could see an old man driving who seemed about as grizzled as the pickup. He scowled as Bud boarded the van, then pulled out after them onto the highway, as if following.

Bud wondered why the old guy would stop, but then decided

maybe he'd intended to give Bud a ride. The scowl was probably just his normal look, Bud thought, though he did find it odd that the guy had been going towards Whitehorse and was now following them the opposite way—or maybe he hadn't been stopping for Bud at all, but just turning around.

Bud looked around the van, noting that it held two adult women in the front—the driver and passenger—and around a dozen girls in the back, all appearing to be around the age of ten to twelve years old. In the very back of the van were backpacks and camping gear stacked almost to the ceiling.

Bud introduced himself, then Lindie, and it was quickly apparent that the girls were interested in the dog. Just as he'd predicted, it appeared that the van had stopped more for Lindie than for him.

Lindie took to all the attention like a duck to water, wagging her tail and visiting each girl in turn, making her way to the back of the van then back again to the front, the girls vying for her attention.

The woman who'd asked Bud where he was going laughed, then introduced herself as Jan, and the driver as Carolyn.

"We're going backpacking up in the Tombstones," Jan said, smiling, turning her captain's seat around to face him. "You're looking at the Whitehorse All-Girls Junior Hockey Team. We're going to spend a night up at Grizzly Lake. It's great for bonding and will help us get in shape for hockey season. Then we're going into Dawson and stay at a lodge for three days."

"The Tombstones?" Bud asked.

Jan replied, "You know, Tombstone Territorial Park, up in the Ogilvies. But it looks like you're going backpacking, too. Where you headed on the Dempster?"

"I'm not really backpacking," Bud replied. "I'm just going to find a nice spot and hang out and take photos of the aurora, assuming it's not too cold."

"The aurora comes out even when it's cold," one of the girls said.

"I'm sure he knows that, Alexsa," Jan replied patiently. "He's talking about too cold for camping."

"Get some silk longjohns," another girl said. "That'll keep you warm."

Now yet another girl asked, "Can we borrow your dog? She'll help keep the bears away. What kind of dog is she, anyway?"

Bud replied, "She's a Carolina dingo, but I don't know much about them."

Now Jan said, "Aren't they the only truly wild dog in America? I read that their DNA is at the base of the family tree for dogs, the most primitive type. They're how a dog would look without all the inter-breeding and selection by humans. They're called Pariah dogs, which are ancient breeds with little or no influence from humans in their evolution. They're supposed to be very smart and loyal."

The girls were all listening, taking turns stroking Lindie.

"How do you know so much about them, Ms. Taylor?" Alexsa asked.

Jan replied, "I read that there's a guy down by Bennett Lake who has a pair and has had a few litters. He says they're very well adapted to the bush. There was an article in the paper not long ago. Is that where you got Lindie?" She asked Bud.

Bud replied, "I didn't get her there, but I was told that's where she came from. She was supposedly named for Lindeman Lake, which is where the fellow lives."

Jan continued, "I read about a guy who drowned down on Bennett Lake recently, and they'd been looking for his dog, a Carolina dingo."

"This is the dog," Bud said. "I found her, and the guy's brother wanted me to keep her."

Jan looked shocked. "This is the dog? The same one?"

"Yes," Bud replied, wondering why she was so surprised. "Did his boat sink?"

Jan now leaned towards Bud and spoke quietly so the girls couldn't hear her. "I shouldn't be telling you this, because I was told it by my boyfriend, who's got a friend in the RCMP, but they think he was murdered. They found his PFD, personal floatation device, and it'd been taken off and was on the beach, but his boat had been flipped and he was floating in the water. His dog went missing, and they thought maybe she'd been taken by whoever killed him. If I recall correctly, his name was William, he was First Nations, and the RCMP thinks it's all connected to another guy who was killed recently up near Dawson, a geologist."

Bud now thought back to Joe and Dan. He knew they were looking for Lindie from Joe's reaction to seeing her, but had they also been looking for someone else? And if they'd suspected Bud of killing William, especially since Bud had Lindie, why had they treated him so well, even letting him spend the night? He thought back to how Dan had asked him if he'd seen anyone else out there. It had almost been like they'd known who they were looking for.

Jan continued, "To be honest with you, we almost cancelled this trip because of it all, but we decided to go ahead, since we'll be far from the road. Carolyn was hesitant to pick you up, but the girls wanted to see the dog."

Bud sighed. "I'm just a simple farmer from Utah who's come up here to take photos of the wilderness and aurora. And actually, if it helps matters any, I also serve as the local sheriff."

As soon as he said it, he wondered if telling it might come back and bite him, but he could see Jan visibly relax.

She said, "You'd be more than welcome to come packing with us. We could use the peace of mind of having a law enforcement officer along, as well as a dog."

Bud was speechless. She didn't know him from Adam, and what if he was the killer in disguise? And knowing what she'd just told him, wasn't it irresponsible of them as guardians of the girls to pick him up in the first place?

As if reading his mind, Jan whispered, "Shorty told me you might be coming, to watch for you—he has a number of people keeping an eye out. That's the real reason we picked you up, though the dog kind of threw us off, as we didn't expect you to have one. He sent me an online article with your photo—you'd won some kind of Utah Sheriff's Association award a few years back, and you looked like the same guy, so we stopped."

Bud sank back in the seat, his turn to be shocked.

14

Bud was still tired from his hike on the railroad tracks along Bennett Lake, and the monotonous drone of the girls' singing was putting him to sleep.

> One hundred bottles of beer on the wall,
> One hundred bottles of beer,
> You take one down, pass it around,
> Ninety-nine bottles of beer on the wall...

He slumped down in his seat, fast asleep, and later woke to:

> The ants go marching two by two, hurrah, hurrah,
> The ants go marching two by two, hurrah, hurrah!
> The ants go marching two by two,
> The little one stopped to tie its shoe,
> And they all go marching down, in the ground, to get
>   out of the rain...

Lindie was somewhere in the back with the girls, Bud figured, as he drifted back to sleep.

He'd wanted to stay awake for the scenery, but when he finally awoke, they were already a number of hours into the drive. He felt somewhat refreshed, and sitting up, noticed that Jan was now sitting by him, Alexsa in the front.

Bud badly wanted a cup of coffee, but he knew the odds of getting one were slim to none, but he decided to ask anyway.

"Any idea where I could get a cup of coffee?"

"We're almost at Moose Creek Lodge. We're going to stop to get a bite to eat. But Bud, like I said, Shorty's got a few people out looking for you, but I don't think that guy following us in that old pickup is one. I think you should lie low. Stay in the van with Lindie, get in the back. I'll bring you out some coffee and something to eat."

Everyone piled out from the van and went inside the old roadhouse. Moose Creek Lodge had been built with logs from the nearby boreal forest and had a large set of moose antlers over the door. Its bright red roof and window trim made it look inviting, and the giant mosquito statues on the lawn added a bit of whimsy. Various burl sculptures sat near antique gas pumps, and a Yukon Territory flag hung from a pole attached to the roof.

Bud watched as the old rusty pickup pulled up nearby and the old guy got out. Lindie sat by Bud's side, also watching the old guy come up to the van, slowly wagging her tail. The guy was wearing dirty coveralls and a blue-jean jacket with holes in the elbows, and the wrinkles in his face made him look like he hadn't been indoors for years. Bud could tell he was First Nations.

Jan had told Bud to lie low, but he figured he'd just as soon know what kind of trouble was following him around than to hide from it.

The man shaded his eyes with his hand and peered into the vehicle.

"Afternoon," Bud said, and the man jumped back, surprised.

"Holy moose eggs, I sure didn't see you," he replied. "Startled me."

"Can I help you with something?" Bud asked.

The man held out his hand to Lindie, who started licking it. Finally, he said, "I thought I recognized Lindie back there. I've been following you forever. What are you doing with Willie's dog? She's been lost, you know."

"How do you know this is the same dog?" Bud asked.

The man shrugged his shoulders, saying, "There's only one dog like this in the Yukon. Everybody else has huskies or mutts. Lindie's one of a kind." The dog continued licking him as he stroked her ruff. "I've spent many hours playing with this dog—Willie's dog."

"You do know William's gone now, don't you?"

"If you mean dead, yes, I know. You're not from around here, but let me tell you that the Yukon's a big place with few people. Word travels fast. There's a reward out for this dog."

The man now looked at Bud as if waiting for an explanation. Bud wondered if the man didn't want the dog just so he could claim the reward, presumably posted by Joe.

Bud replied, "It's pretty simple. I found the dog, and William's brother gave her to me. She was down on Bennett Lake. I guess that's where William drowned."

"I just can't picture Joe giving the dog away to a stranger, and we think Willie was killed, he didn't drown."

"I thought that was proprietary information, and the RCMP didn't want everyone knowing that," Bud replied, hoping the old man knew something about William's murder. For some reason, he had a hunch it tied in with the murder of the geologist, just like Jan had said.

The old man again shrugged his shoulders. "Like I said, everyone in the Yukon knows about everything around here. No secrets."

Bud now asked, "You play chess?"

"What's that got to do with anything?"

"Never mind. I just feel like we're playing some kind of game. Look, Joe gave me the dog."

The old man hesitated, then said, "I'm Stanley Walker. I've got a roadhouse on up the highway a ways. I don't get out much, but I was on my way to Whitehorse for supplies when I saw the dog. Now I've got to turn around and go back all that ways, a big waste of gas, I can tell you, which I can't afford. But I'd sure like to take Lindie with me. I can contact Joe and see if what you're saying is true or not."

For some reason Bud suspected this man knew more about the goings on in the country than he would want anyone to know. On a hunch, Bud asked, "Do you know a fellow named Shorty Doyle?"

The man looked at the ground and said, "Everybody knows Shorty. Why do you want to know?"

Suddenly, Bud remembered the names Stanley and Lily. He said, "You're Joe's dad, aren't you? And your wife is Lily, and your roadhouse is the Klondike Cafe. And you do know Shorty—and you probably also know where he is."

Now Stanley frowned. "You sure know a lot for being a stranger. Are you a Mountie?"

Bud laughed. He could now see everyone coming out from the cafe.

"I'm Bud Shumway. Shorty sent for me and told me to find you guys, but it looks like you found me instead."

Stanley looked directly at Bud, who thought he could see a lifetime of hard work and even sorrow and disappointment in his eyes.

Stanley now said, "I'm going back to Whitehorse. If your ride's going by the cafe, have them drop you and Lindie off there. If not, get out at the junction with the Dempster and walk about 2 kilometers up the highway. Go around to the back door. Lily won't answer unless you yell, so don't bother to knock, she's hard of hearing. Tell her you have Lindie, and she'll open the door."

With that, the old guy turned and walked away, back to his pickup, Bud wondering if the ancient beat-up vehicle would even make it back to Whitehorse.

15

"Just how far is two kilometers in miles?" Bud asked Alexsa, who was sitting by him, Lindie in the middle.

"Hmmm, I think it's about 10 miles," Alexsa replied.

Jan laughed. "Wrong answer. One kilometer is approximately 0.6 miles. Here's a little trick: to convert kilometers to miles, divide the number by 2 and add 10% of the original number. Makes it pretty easy."

"So, that means when I see a sign for 100 kilometers, I divide by two and get 50, then add 10% of 100, which is 10, and I get 60 miles, right?" Bud asked.

"Very good," Jan replied. "So, two kilometers is about 1.2 miles. Why do you ask?"

"Just trying to think like a Canadian," Bud grinned.

He was feeling much better after his long nap and a tuna sandwich made with freshly baked bread, a cup of hearty homemade soup, and a fresh salad from the Moose Creek Lodge. It was the first real food he'd had for some time, and the strawberry tart he'd had for dessert was delicious. He wondered if somehow Wilma Jean could call them and get the recipe.

He now began to worry, knowing his wife and probably Howie

also were starting to wonder about him, since he hadn't called recently. He knew that things probably weren't going to get any better, as they seemed to be getting into more and more remote country.

His thoughts were interrupted by one of the girls behind him saying, "Mr. Shumway, did you know that the Yukon River is 3520 kilometers long, the 4th longest in the world?"

Bud laughed. "Let's see if I can do the math. Let's see...that's around 2112 miles. Am I close?"

"How'd you do that so fast?" The girl asked.

Bud held up his phone. "I have a calculator on it. I just multiplied 3520 by six-tenths."

Now another girl said, "Did you know that there were more than 250 sternwheelers on the Yukon River from 1896 to the mid 1950s?"

Bud laughed. "I thought this was a hockey team, not a trivia team. But I have one for you guys, what's a cheechako?"

One said, "It's a kind of monkey."

The other woman, Carolyn, who'd been driving but had now switched off with Jan, said, "It's a newcomer."

"Not an ignoramus?" Bud asked.

"Well, I guess a newcomer might be ignorant of things, since they're new, but actually, no. It was a term used during the gold rush. Those who had been here at least one winter were called sourdoughs. The terms stuck and are still used."

Some of the girls in the back were now having a heated argument, and Bud listened in.

"Hank Yarbo's the best, not Lacey! She's way too prissy."

"I think Davis is best. And yeah, Lacy's a wimp."

"What about Oscar?"

"He's too acerbic."

"What's acerbic? Why don't you use normal words?"

"I dunno, it's just what my mom always says about Oscar."

Bud turned to Carolyn and asked, "What are they arguing about?"

She replied, "It's a TV show called *Corner Gas*. It revolves around a gas station on the prairie in Saskatchewan."

Bud laughed. "Sounds exciting."

"It's actually a great show," she replied. "It's very popular."

The girls were now discussing hockey moves, and Bud quietly asked Carolyn, "What's going on with Shorty Doyle? Do you know?"

She said, "We got to know Shorty through the hockey league. He's a big donor. Jan and I both work for the recreation district and became good friends with him. Shorty's very popular in Whitehorse. He donates to all kinds of causes and is a very likable guy."

She leaned back, then continued. "Whitehorse isn't all that big, around 26,000 people, most of the population of the Yukon, and we all know each other. There was a government geologist named Luke Anderson who lived in Dawson for many years. He recently went missing, and the Mounties supposedly found evidence that he'd been murdered, though no one knows what that evidence is exactly, as they're being very tight-lipped about it all, which they should be when a case is active. But they've been after Shorty for the murder, though they can't exactly arrest him, since there's no body yet. Shorty's taking no chances and is hiding out."

"Why do they think he would murder Anderson?"

"Shorty and Anderson have had a feud going for years."

"A feud? Over what?"

"Shorty made his claim to fame as a geologist by discovering the oldest rocks in the world. He spent a lot of time in the bug-infested bush north of Yellowknife in the Northwest Territories. Then Anderson did him one better and spent time even farther north and found rock that's supposedly even more ancient. It's a scientific feud, but the Mounties are viewing it as motive to kill. The two have had some heated arguments in conferences and such, so I've been told, and almost came to blows. Anderson apparently had no known enemies, so the Mounties are looking at Shorty."

Bud was quiet, wondering again why Shorty had contacted him after so many years. What was he supposed to do? And why had Shorty sent him a mining claim? None of it made sense, especially the part where Shorty had told Cassie that his life was at stake. Canada didn't have the death penalty, did it?

"How do you know him?" Carolyn asked.

"He was my high-school science teacher back in Utah."

Carolyn looked surprised. "High school? In the States?"

Bud replied, "Shorty was born and raised in my hometown of Green River, Utah. His mom was Canadian, so he has dual citizenship. I guess he came up here after teaching at Stanford for awhile. The call of the wild and all that."

"He's an ivy leaguer? Shorty?"

"I don't know anything about that, just that he went to Stanford and got a PhD, then taught there."

"And you stayed in touch all those years?"

"No, but he stayed in contact with our current high-school science teacher, and called her when all this came down."

"And you came up here to help Shorty? What are you going to do?"

"I don't know the answer to that question," Bud replied quietly. "I wish I did."

They sat and watched the scenery for awhile. Bud was amazed at how beautiful it was, but in a way completely different than what he would've guessed. The tall glaciated mountains had gradually mellowed out into rolling hills.

Now Bud pulled out his harmonica. Lindie was asleep next to him, her nose resting on his leg.

He asked Carolyn, "You mind if I play? I'm just learning, but it helps sooth my nerves a little. Besides, it'll be my way of torturing the girls for singing *One Hundred Bottles of Beer on the Wall*.

Carolyn laughed and nodded her approval.

Bud started with his old favorite, *Red River Valley*, deciding *Ghost Riders* was too technical, then segued into *Tennessee Waltz*, then on to the new song he was working on, which he'd decided to call *The Yukon Trail*.

After awhile, he stopped to take a break and looked around.

Everyone in the van except Jan, who was driving, was sound asleep, including Carolyn, who was using Lindie as a pillow.

16

"Lily, hello! Anybody home?"

Bud stood in front of the Klondike Cafe, wondering if he had the right place, as the cafe sign had apparently either been taken down or had fallen down. The building was old and weatherworn and didn't look like anyone had lived there for years, except maybe a marmot or two.

The old roadhouse was boarded up with signs nailed over the windows that read "Keep Out," "Private Property," and even included an upside-down "No Trespassing" sign, but nowhere did it say "Klondike Cafe." Weeds grew everywhere, and the parking lot was littered with old rusted diesel barrels, which Bud figured had been used to run the generator.

Bud yelled again, then decided to go around to the rear of the building, since the front door looked like it was forever sealed with time.

The Whitehorse All-Girls Junior Hockey Team had dropped Bud and Lindie off a half-mile or so down the road so as to decrease the odds of anyone following and seeing where he was going. He'd slunk through the trees until reaching the old roadhouse, hiding his pack in the nearby bushes.

The back looked more promising with a door that actually looked usable. Bud again yelled, remembering that Stanley had said Lily was somewhat deaf.

Now the door opened a crack and he heard a woman say, "Lindie! Is that really you, Lindie?"

The little dog was beside herself, running to the door and wagging her tail. The door opened, and Lindie went inside, then it closed again.

Bud stood there for a moment, figuring that it would soon open again, but when it didn't he started yelling again, frustrated.

"Lily, it's Bud, Shorty's friend. I talked to Stanley, and he said you'd be here. Can I come in?"

His words echoed a bit, and Bud suddenly felt very vulnerable, as if the whole world could hear him. What good had it done him to come to the Klondike Cafe when they wouldn't even let him in?

Now the door slowly opened a crack, and a woman's voice asked, "Are you the guy with the harmonica?"

Bud was surprised. His musical reputation seemed to be spreading across Canada.

"That would be me," he answered. "Can I come in?"

The door opened, and a small wiry woman grinned mischievously, waving him inside. She had gray hair in a long braid down her back and wore a colorful but simple cotton dress that almost looked like she'd converted it from a nightgown by sewing on sleeves. Around her neck was a somewhat stately necklace bearing four large bear claws, which Bud thought looked incongruous against her flowered dress. Her wrinkles almost matched those of her husband, Stanley, but she had a more optimistic air about her.

Bud was surprised to see how comfortable and clean the cafe's interior was. It looked just as it probably had when they closed it, he mused, with tables and chairs and menus and even a juke box in the corner, but it now had books and newspapers neatly arranged on the tables, along with clothes and coats and hats hanging on hooks along the walls. In the corner was an old rusty barrel stove, with several chairs nearby and shelves along the back.

"Welcome, Mr. Utah," Lily said, still smiling. "Shorty will be very happy to hear you've finally arrived. We thought you would never get here."

Bud nodded agreeably, trying to figure out exactly how long it had been since he'd left home. He was surprised to realize it had only been three days. It felt like weeks, but then, he'd seen a lot of country, he figured.

"I think I'm making pretty good time for not having a car," he replied.

"You seem like a very ingenious fellow. My brother Walt called a friend in Dawson who drove out here to tell me you were coming. He said to tease you about your harmonica. Thank you for finding Lindie."

Lily now seemed sad, and Bud knew it must be hard to lose one's son, especially through mindless violence.

"Lindie's pretty special," he said.

"Yes, and I think she'll be happy here with us."

Bud was surprised, seeing how Joe had given the dog to him. But it did make sense for Lily and Stanley to keep her. After all, she'd belonged to their son and probably had special associations for them.

As if to emphasize what he was thinking, Lily added, "I have many fond memories watching Willie play with this dog. She was his best friend."

Bud was now having trouble not feeling disappointed. He knew it was for the best, as it would probably be hard for him to get her across the border—heck, it was going to be hard getting himself back across the border.

He knew the U.S. border agent would question why he was returning from a country he hadn't legally entered, and with the electronic tracking they now had with passports, they would surely know. It would make things much more difficult if he tried to take Lindie back with him.

He now asked, "Where's Shorty?"

Lily replied, "Stanley should be home before too long. He went to Whitehorse. Did you say you talked to him?"

"He's going to be a few hours later than he might," Bud replied, explaining how Stanley had followed them partway back.

"If that's the case, he probably won't be back until tomorrow. He'll have to find his brother and beg some gas money. But grab a chair and tell me a little about yourself. Want some tea? Are you hungry?"

Bud smiled, sitting down in an old well-worn rocker. "I'm OK, but Lindie might be hungry. I have some dog food for her in my pack, but I hid it back in the bushes. I'll go get it. But is Shorty staying here?"

Lily gave him an odd look. "Stanley lives here with me."

Bud tried again. "*Shorty*, Lily, I said *Shorty*, not *Stanley*."

"I heard you the first time," she replied. "Tea?"

"Sure, that sounds good," Bud now whispered.

"You take cream and sugar? I hope not, because we don't have either," Lily asked.

"I have some in my pack," Bud whispered even more softly.

"I know what you're doing, buster," Lily laughed. "You think I have selective hearing, don't you? Stan thinks I can't hear much of anything, but just between you and me, I can hear just fine."

"When you want to, eh?" Bud grinned.

"Go get your pack. I haven't had cream and sugar in my tea for years."

Bud slipped out the door, hoping he could find where he'd stashed his pack, Lindie following.

17

Even though the cream Bud promised turned out to be powdered milk, Lily seemed happy enough as she and Bud sat by the old barrel stove working on their second cups of tea. It was getting late, and the fire was low, and even though Bud was again tired, he was like a little kid, wanting to stay awake and not miss anything.

Lily's stories of the people and history of the area were fascinating, and Bud knew he was hearing things from the view of a First Nations member, something rarely shared with non-natives.

Bud had in turn told her all about the dogs and his wife and their farm. There was something about the old woman that made him open up—maybe her unconditional approval and interest, and she seemed to genuinely like him.

Bud now asked, "Lily, do you have any kids besides Joe and William?"

She replied, "Yes, I have a daughter down in Horsefly, down by Williams Lake in B.C. She married a guy from down there. He travels a lot, as he's a high-angle worker."

"What's that?"

"I'm not sure. All I know is he climbs towers and big buildings and fixes things for people. He makes good money. They have two kids, but I seldom get to see them."

"That's too bad," Bud replied. "But you never go down there?"

"I would love to go stay with them some, but I can never afford it. My daughter offers to send travel money, but I don't want to leave Stan, and he won't go. His health's not too good."

Bud nodded, and Lily continued.

"We used to make good money here, well, maybe not good, but enough. We served food and had gas pumps and a tire service. Life's been pretty hard since then—not to complain—and Stan makes a little from gold panning on the river, but we just barely get by. To be honest, I don't know what's going to become of us. I hope we don't end up like Grady."

"Grady?"

"Yeah, Grady Johnson. He worked for us, and when we shut down, he had nowhere to go. He tried getting a job in Dawson, but he's a hard luck kind of guy and nobody would hire him. We let him stay here for awhile after we closed, but he drifted on. The cafe closing really affected him mentally, and last I heard he'd kind of gone off the deep end. He was begging on the streets of Whitehorse, living out of his old Willys pickup."

"Why did you shut down?"

"Same old government nonsense."

Lily was silent for awhile, and Bud was beginning to think she didn't want to talk about it. She got up and put more wood in the barrel stove, then settled back into her big faded-leather recliner, pulled her gray wool blanket around her, and said, "You may have noticed how close we are to the river. When Stan and I built the cafe, the river was at least a hundred yards farther to the east. Most of these old roadhouses were built using whatever was on hand, and ours was no different. They all ran on generators and used septic systems, some of which were pretty primitive."

She shifted in her chair getting more comfortable, then continued. "The Canadian government didn't originally pay much mind to the Yukon, but after so many years, after we became a territory, they started coming around and meddling in everything. The river shifted closer to us, which is pretty common for these big rivers. Their government toady came by one day and told us we had to upgrade our septic system, as we were too close to the river and were violating environmental protection laws. The upgrades would've cost us more than everything we'd ever made from the cafe. We didn't have that kind of money, so we had to shut it all down."

"Is this the Klondike River?" Bud asked.

"It's the North Klondike River, its headwaters are kind of to the northeast of here. It flows into the Klondike, which then flows into the Yukon at Dawson."

Bud asked, "If you sold gas, where are the pumps?"

Lily replied, "Gulf Canada, which used to be B/A Oil, came and took them after we closed. We owned those pumps, but they took them anyway. When we opened the roadhouse, B/P installed the tanks and we paid them five cents a gallon until the pumps were paid off—this was back before Canada went metric in the early 1970s and went to liters. We'd paid them in full years ago, and they basically stole them from us. After that, there was no way we could reopen. We even filled up an occasional bush plane from them pumps."

Lily paused, then said, "What was a bitter pill was that after we closed, they opened an unmanned gas station just down the road at the intersection of the Dempster and Klondike highways. They would've taken all our business anyway. But in some ways it was good riddance to the whole shebang. You get your fill of tourists. You get ten good ones and one pain in the ass, and the pain in the ass ruins your whole day."

She then laughed, as if remembering. "But man, people loved my cooking. I was so busy, one summer I used seven tons of flour—can you imagine how many cinnamon rolls that made? Seven tons of flour. I'd make 25 dozen cinnamon rolls a day and a hundred loaves of bread, and all kinds of pastries and meat pies. I eventually even added pizzas, doughnuts, tarts, turnovers, and cookies. I fed tourists and townsfolk, and a lot of gold miners. But my best and most famous was my Berry Delight pie. I'd start my day at three in the morning, and the only time I ever took off was when I had to have some teeth pulled. We were open for 28 years, and I estimate I made over three-million cinnamon rolls. You'd work your rear off in the summer and take the winter off."

The fire was nearly out, and Bud was starting to get sleepy. Lily added nostalgically, "It was a good life. We even fed the Mounties, often for free. Back then, they didn't get any per diem, and we had many a Mountie sleep on our couch, and we'd serve them a free breakfast. We felt like it was our way of helping make the countryside safer. You have no idea of the lawlessness that went on back then— and the roadhouse owners were often the worst. They would burn each other out, shoot at each other, even put up 'road washed out' signs to keep travelers around for an extra day or two. When the Mounties started coming around, things got much better. My son Willie was a Mountie, you know. I was very proud of him."

Bud was surprised and said, "I didn't know that."

Lily nodded in the gathering darkness, the fire now out. "About the only good that came out of the cafe closing was that Grady finally left."

Bud asked, "Why was that good?"

"Well, he came into this country from down around Carcross, and everybody down there had known him since he was a kid. But we left Carcross years ago, and we didn't know anything about him, or we would've never hired him in the first place. He's First Nations, like us, and we try to help each other out, so we gave him a job when he came by asking. It didn't take long to notice he was different, but Stan was afraid of him by then, afraid to fire him, so we let him stay on. As long as everything went well, he was OK and a good hard worker, but if anything went even a little astray, he would get weird. Stan said his brain was wired different—he couldn't deal with stress of any kind."

Bud asked, "What did he do?"

"He would start getting irritable and drink. One time he actually pointed a long gun at some poor tourist who had complained that Grady hadn't fixed his tire right. Stan had to get involved in that, and he swore he was going to fire him, but he never did. You always wondered when something might set Grady off, he even shot the pay phone off the wall once, and we haven't had a phone since. Though he never did actually harm anyone, I do know he started hurting our business. People going north up to Eagle Plains and Inuvik would normally stop here rather than having to go on into Dawson, but people started avoiding us. Stan and I had many a pillow talk over how to get rid of Grady, but the government came in and shut us down and solved the problem."

She now paused, and Bud thought she was done, but she soon added, "I've been told that he gets on the riverside trolly there in Whitehorse and rides back and forth, begging from tourists and harassing them, and he's been arrested for vagrancy several times. I'm glad he's gone, and he'd better not come back. But I just wish I could go on down to Vickie's in Horsefly and forget this place. My son Joe told me I could come down there, but they really don't have room."

She sighed, then said, "But that's enough of the good old days. I'm gonna go to bed. You can sleep anywhere you want, as long as it's on the floor."

Bud replied, "I really want to thank you for putting me up, but do you know where Shorty is?"

"He should be by shortly," she replied. "He's overdue to check in and resupply, though it won't do much good if Stan doesn't get back from Whitehorse. Better get some rest while you can."

Lily got up and disappeared into a back room, then, as if changing her mind, returned and said, "Mr. Utah, would you mind playing your harmonica for a bit? I can hear it in the bedroom, and it would be really nice to go to sleep by. My dad used to play harmonica for us kids at bedtime."

Bud grinned, then replied, "Sure, but don't get your hopes up for anything special. I'm just starting to learn it."

He laid out his sleeping pad on the floor near the stove and sat cross-legged on his bag, still in his clothes, leaning against the wall, with Lindie at his feet.

Pulling out his harmonica, Bud played every tune he knew, which didn't take long, then started over again, gradually slumping down against the wall until, dropping the harmonica, he was fast asleep in the dim glow of the still-hot metal stove.

18

Bud stood on the bank of the North Klondike River, trying to figure out how to use a sluice box, if that was indeed what the long wooden thing in front of him was.

Shorty had told him it was a matter of life and death for him to get at least an ounce of gold from it, and he had only a few hours to do so, but Shorty, who had then conveniently disappeared, hadn't told him how to operate the dang thing. Bud knew he was going to give him a bad grade when he came back.

Lindie was at his feet, and Bud wondered if she was hungry, as he couldn't remember if he'd fed her that morning or not. In fact, he couldn't remember if he himself had had breakfast or not. And come to think of it, what had happened to his pack with the dog food in it? No wonder they hadn't eaten, he didn't have any food.

Now he thought he saw a large dark form in the nearby willows, a form shaped just like a big grizzly—or was it Shorty? No, Shorty was tall, but not bulky, and this thing was tall and wide.

Now Lindie was on her stomach, head down, as if trying to make herself smaller. Bud was surprised, as he'd heard that Carolina dingos were brave and fearless dogs, but so much for that myth, he thought.

Suddenly, Lindie threw herself into the air at the dark form, which had quickly emerged from the willows and was coming for Bud.

"Call the dog off!" The bear growled, which totally threw Bud for a loop. It again growled, "Call the dog!"

Strangely enough, the bear sounded just like a man! How could this be?

He now heard a woman saying, "Lindie, get over here and be good!" The voice sounded just like Lily.

Bud turned over and sat up. He'd been dreaming, and he could now see Lily in her robe, holding Lindie by the collar, as a tall thin man stood nearby in the shadows. Lily lit an oil lamp, and as Bud woke up, everything became clear.

Shorty had come during the night, just as Lily had said he might, and Lindie, thinking he was a stranger, had done her job of trying to protect them.

Now Shorty called softly to the dog, and Lily released her. Lindie went first to Bud, who assured her it was OK, then hesitantly went to Shorty, who bent down and patted her head.

"Man, what a good guard dog you are," he said. "Isn't this Willie's dog?"

Lily replied, "Yes, and this is Bud, AKA Mr. Utah, the fellow you sent for. Mr. Utah, I give you Shorty, AKA Jacob Doyle."

Bud stood, still in his clothes from the day before, and shook Shorty's hand.

"It's been a few years," Bud said.

"It has indeed," Shorty replied. "Thanks for coming."

"It was nothing," Bud replied.

Lily snorted. "If that's *nothing*, I'd like to see what *something* is. He came by jet, float plane, train, foot, truck, and with a hockey team. Can you imagine all that as nothing?"

Bud grinned. "Well, it took very little effort on my part—except for the on foot section, anyway."

Shorty now sat down at one of the cafe tables and asked, "Lily, is Stan back? I don't see his truck."

"Nope, and he won't be until later this evening, I would guess," she replied. "He waylaid himself chasing Mr. Utah halfway back here from Whitehorse, thinking he'd found Lindie, then had to turn around. I know he probably went on down to Carcross and borrowed money from Walt or maybe Joe, cause he didn't have any gas money."

"I thought I gave him plenty of money," Shorty said with concern. "I don't expect him to run around on my behalf for free."

"I know, I know," Lily said, frustrated. "But he forgot to tell you he owed a back bill to the station and they wouldn't pump him any gas until he paid it. He called a friend from Whitehorse who ran out here and told me all this. He got the supplies, but needed gas money."

"You mean the station down the road here at the Klondike Highway?"

"No, that one's credit cards only, there's no attendant, you know that. The one at this end of Dawson—they've been extending us credit. Shorty, we're going to have to do something soon. We just can't continue on like this."

"You mean helping supply me?" Shorty asked.

"No, that's the only thing keeping us going. It's just everything in general. Stan's old truck needs new CV joints, and we can't even afford to buy the parts so he can fix it."

Bud sat back quietly, listening, amazed at how little Shorty had changed since being his high-school teacher. He was a tall man, handsome, his red hair streaked with gray, with a square jaw and sparkling eyes. Bud couldn't picture him killing anything or anyone.

He wondered if Shorty had talked to Cassie lately. He was becoming more and more concerned at the lack of communication with his wife and everyone back home, as he knew they must be worried.

"I'm not sure I should stay here all day waiting for him," Shorty said. "Though I badly need those supplies. Are you pretty sure he'll be back today?"

"He knows you're waiting. But it is risky. It would be lots cheaper and faster if he didn't have to go to Whitehorse for stuff."

Shorty replied, "I know, but I also know someone in Dawson would eventually notice how you guys seem to have money all of a sudden, buying supplies, and then they'd put two and two together. But Bud, do you think anyone possibly caught on to where you were going?"

Bud shook his head no. "I'm not even in Canada legally, Shorty. I don't even think the RCMP knows I'm here."

He then told Shorty about Dougie McDougald's visit to Green River, as well as the woman on the plane, then about how he'd managed to find his way to the Yukon.

Shorty shook his head. "I'd heard you were good, but that's beyond my expectations."

"All accidental," he replied. "Nothing to do with skill. Just a combination of bumbling luck."

"And he even found Lindie," Lily added. "I think he has a guardian angel."

"Maybe two or three," Shorty grinned. "But if I have even one, it's probably on high alert right now. Bud, we think the RCMP has linked me to Lily and Stan, and may even be checking the Klondike Cafe occasionally. I don't want to implicate them in anything, but they're the only way I know of to get supplies. We need to get going. I have enough for a couple more days, so we'll be back, Lily."

"I wish I could go," she said.

"Be happy you're not," Shorty replied. "I'm camping in some pretty rough country, and it's getting cold at night. I don't know what I'm going to do if we can't resolve all this before winter hits, and it's coming soon. My big water jug froze solid last night"

Shorty stood to go, and Bud put his sleeping bag in its stuff sack and rolled up his pad, putting everything in his backpack.

"I assume she's going with me," Bud said as he grabbed Lindie's leash.

"I think she'd be better off here," Lily said. "Too many bears out there. Stan and I want to keep her."

Bud sighed and handed Lily the leash. "You're right, but I'll miss her."

He took her dog food from his pack, then patted her head and turned to Lily. "Be sure to give her a Barkie Biscuit every once in awhile."

As he and Shorty walked out the door into the darkness, a slight iridescent trace of green aurora glowed to the north, but Bud was too sleepy to notice.

19

Bud nearly walked into Shorty's vehicle in the dark, but Shorty grabbed him by the arm and guided him to the vehicle's passenger door, whispering, "Don't talk. Throw your pack in the back, then help me push. Be ready to jump in when it starts rolling."

Bud did as he was told, and when the vehicle started moving, he could feel it sink a little as Shorty jumped in the driver's side, and he was soon inside also, pulling the door shut. He could now tell they were in an old Ford pickup.

They rolled silently down the gradually sloped drive of the Klondike Cafe and onto the highway, continuing on the road with no lights until Shorty suddenly popped the clutch, making the engine roar to life.

"How did you keep from running off the road?" Bud asked with concern.

"I wanted to get away some before making any noise. The road's pretty straight here, so you just need to keep the steering wheel lined up."

Bud didn't say anything. He knew if he were staking out a place, he would know if a vehicle was there or not, even if it was dark and it came and went with the engine off. But since Shorty was a geologist, maybe he wasn't aware of things like night-vision goggles and such.

As if reading his mind, Shorty said, "I know that down in the States you can watch a place pretty effectively, but I'm banking on the RCMP being short-handed in these parts. They probably have no idea Lily and Stan are supplying me, but even if they did, they can't really arrest me yet, or so I think, knock on wood."

"Why not? Didn't they accuse you of murder?"

"Yes, and they're quite serious, but they don't have a body. You can't prove murder without a body."

"No body?"

"Nope. I'll explain later. Right now, could you reach in the back and find a thermos? It has coffee in it. Pour yourself a cup in the lid, then I can just drink from the thermos, since I only have one cup."

"I actually have a metal cup I bought in Whitehorse," Bud said, reaching back and finding the thermos, then feeling in his backpack for his cup. He then pulled a headlamp from his pack and filled the thermos lid, handing it to Shorty, then pouring himself a cup.

"What's that say on your cup?" Shorty asked as the light illuminated it.

"Bigfoot, Whitehorse, Y.T.," Bud answered.

"Bigfoot? They call it Sasquatch up here," Shorty said. "They must've made the cup down in the States. You believe in Sasquatch?"

"No, but maybe in Bigfoot," Bud smiled, thinking back to when he'd maybe actually seen one, long ago, up near the Ghost Rock Cafe out of Green River.

Bud was suddenly homesick. He wondered what the boys were doing and hoped Wilma Jean was giving them their Barkie Biscuits. He then thought of Lindie and how quickly he'd become attached to her, thinking he might be able to take her home, only to have his hopes dashed, though he knew it was probably for the best. His thoughts then turned to Howie and Maureen, and he wondered how she was doing with the pregnancy.

"You know about that, don't you?" Shorty asked Bud.

"What? Know about what?"

Shorty sighed. "I know you must be tired, but I was saying that Anderson's buried in a rock avalanche, and I don't think they're ever going to find his body, but they're also saying they have evidence to tie me to Willie's murder."

"Who's Anderson?" Bud asked.

"Luke Anderson, the geologist who was supposedly murdered up here."

"Why do you say supposedly?" Bud asked.

"Because he's buried in an avalanche. It's rare, but geologists do occasionally die in avalanches. It's one of the risks of the profession, though a negligible one."

Bud, still half asleep, asked, "Where are we going?"

"I have a camp up in the Tombstones. It's about 71 klicks, or kilometers, from the Klondike Cafe to where I park. Anderson and I were doing geological work up there, and I want to finish it up before winter hits." He paused, then added, "I can't go home, anyway."

"You were working together?" Bud asked with surprise.

"Why not?" Shorty asked.

"Someone said you were enemies, that's partly why you're a suspect."

Shorty laughed. "I think they misunderstood. We're feudsters, not enemies."

"You were having a feud, but were friends?"

"Pretty much. We were having a scientific feud, but it wasn't anything personal. We were colleagues, yet competitors. That's how science gets done. You have your theory, and I have mine, and you try to prove yours, and I try to prove mine. The one with the most factual evidence ends up in the books. But we weren't enemies, like Cope and Marsh."

"Who's that?"

"The Dino Wars guys back in the 1800s. They both had hired guys looking all over for dinosaur bones and wanted nothing more than to one up each other. Some good science came out of it, but some bad science did, also. For example, the beast called Brontosaurus had the wrong head put on him in the museum, and it was years before anyone found out it was a mistake."

"Then why would people think you and Anderson were enemies?" Bud asked.

"Well, if you'd gone to some of the geology conferences we were at, you might think that. We had some pretty good arguments, but that's really not uncommon. You should've seen some of the near fisticuffs at tectonic conferences until the evidence gradually proved tectonics was true. Anderson said he had evidence for having the oldest rock on Earth, but he used radiometric dating, which isn't as accurate as using zircon dating, which I used. I can tell you more about that later, if you're interested. But we also collaborated on things. I've been actually helping him with a government geologic survey up here. He and I both worked for the Yukon Geological Survey at one point, though I quit and he didn't. I certainly have no motive for wanting him dead."

"Do you know anyone who did?" Bud asked.

"No. Not a soul. He was a good guy."

Looking out into the darkness, Bud now felt like he was at the end of the Earth. Even back home in the Big Empty one still saw the occasional car light in the distance or even the lights of jets high above. But here, there was nothing, just a blackness that felt as old and ancient as the rocks Shorty had found. He had a strong urge to pull out his harmonica.

They rode on in silence until Bud asked, "How much farther?"

Shorty replied, "We're almost there. It's near Tombstone Territorial Park. Wait till you see it—it's called the Patagonia of Canada for all its spires and jagged peaks. The traditional First Nations' name for the range means 'among ragged-peaked mountains.' It's quite the privilege to be able to work there, and it's also quite the place to get killed. I think Anderson would approve of his resting place."

"So, you don't think he was murdered?" Bud asked.

"I don't know," Shorty replied. "If someone did, they were a lot better with explosives than I am, to bring down an avalanche with such precision. I thought I heard an explosion right before the slide, but the wind was blowing so hard I'm not sure. It could've been the rocks coming loose."

Bud could now see the faint outline of huge spires ahead, barely backlit by the first light of dawn. He could also see that the Dempster Highway was now on an elevated roadbed, and Bud knew that it had been built up to keep the permafrost beneath from melting.

"Shorty, why did you ask me to come up here? What do you think I can do to help you?"

Shorty was silent for awhile, then finally replied, "Bud, I remembered you from school, that one fateful year that your parents sent you to Green River to live with relatives. You were a good kid, one of the best there, smart and good-hearted, and you seemed more centered than the other kids or something. After I left, I would read the news from back home, as I missed Green River. I would've stayed if there'd been the kind of work there I wanted to do, but I wanted to be a field geologist, not a teacher."

Bud grinned, then said, "I'll never forget some of your science experiments, especially the Vesuvius one."

Shorty laughed, then slowed as a red fox ran across the road. "Sometimes I wonder if I made the right decision, and I've always imagined myself retiring back on my parents' little farm there, which I still own and lease out. So I wasn't surprised when I read on the Internet that you'd won a prestigious award from the Utah Sheriff's Association. The article had a photo, and you looked pretty much just like I remembered you. I'd also heard through the years of cases you'd solved, and I felt like you would be the one person who could help me. I knew you were a straight shooter, and we came from the same culture and background. I actually didn't expect you to come. But you can't solve anything out here. This is just an orientation, then you need to go to Dawson."

"What's in Dawson?"

"I don't know, but I don't see how you could solve anything out here in the bush."

"Isn't this where Anderson died?" Bud asked.

Shorty looked directly at Bud and said, "There's an old Robert

Service poem that goes:"

> There are strange things done in the midnight sun,
> By the men who moil for gold;
> The Arctic trails have their secret tales,
> That would make your blood run cold.

"That strangeness pretty much always revolves around humans, Bud, and I'm the only human out here right now, other than you, and I'm innocent. If you can figure out what happened without leaving the bush, then you have my utmost admiration."

"I'll do my best," Bud replied. "But how can I prove you're innocent?"

"By finding the murderer. Even if Anderson wasn't murdered, someone killed Willie, and I'm a suspect for that, too."

Bud was quiet, then said, "I do have to get home before too long."

"I need to get home, too, Bud," Shorty said almost mournfully. "And winter's coming soon here to the Arctic—too soon. We don't have much time."

"We're in the Arctic?" Bud asked.

"We're technically in the sub-Arctic, but the Arctic's not far. The Dempster Highway turnoff is only about 400 klicks from the Arctic Circle—that would be about 240 miles—and we've come about 30 miles of that. This road goes on past the Circle on up to Inuvik in the Northwest Territories and finally ends at Tuktoyaktuk. It used to be an ice road, but they finished the highway this past year. Now it's gravel all the way."

With that, he pulled off the highway onto an almost indiscernible turnoff and drove the Ford into some willows. They got out, and Shorty pulled a green camouflage net over the vehicle, then said, "Follow me."

Bud lifted the pack onto his shoulders and followed, the dawn gradually revealing a mysterious and imposing world of spires, Bud wondering what he would do if Shorty turned out to be guilty after all.

20

After about 15 minutes of bushwhacking, battling tangles of willow and scrub birch, Bud and Shorty dropped into a drainage with a small creek that cut through a thick boreal forest.

There, in a small clearing near the creek, sat a canvas wall tent. The creek provided water, and a portable camp table held a camp stove and a few pots and pans with a large water jug nearby. Shorty had somehow rolled an old barrel into the camp to use as a bear box for food storage. Bud could see a thin layer of frost covering it all.

"Throw your pack in the tent, but be sure and take out anything with an odor first and put it in the barrel," Shorty directed Bud. "I'm surprised it's where I left it. I usually come back to find a bear's messed with it. They roll it around trying to break in. One time it totally disappeared, and I found it a quarter mile away, all dented up, but with the lid still on. They mess around with my pots and pans, too, even though I keep them clean. I've even had a few disappear. They should be mostly hibernating by now, but you never know when a hanger-on will come in."

Trying to not think of what Shorty had just told him, Bud pulled the food from his pack, then took out the small daypack with his camera. "Do you care if I take some photos out here?" He asked. "I'm kind of a photography bug."

"No, go ahead," Shorty replied. "I always think I should get a camera, but I hate to carry more stuff around than I have to. Maybe you can send me some photos when we get back out of here."

Since one side of the camp was against a small hill, Bud decided to climb up to get a better panoramic view. He was soon out of the trees and walking across thick, spongy tundra. Finally on top, he was amazed at a distant view of what he took to be the Tombstone Range, its tall ridges like a huge serrated knife.

He could see a thick cloud cover was coming in, and he wondered exactly where the girls' hockey team was camped. He knew they'd gone up the road to hike to Grizzly Lake, but it was feasible that the trail had cut back into the mountains towards Shorty's camp.

Even though the sun was now up, the light still had that ethereal quality that Bud had noted before. A slight breeze was blowing, making everything chilly, and he knew Shorty was right about them not having much time before winter hit.

Bud took a number of photos, always scanning for bears and other wildlife, and even though he was tired, he felt that elation he always felt when out in the natural world, especially in spectacular landscapes like this.

As he turned to hike back down the hill, he noticed something moving in the breeze, caught in a small tundra plant. He stooped and picked it up—it was a Baby Ruth candy-bar wrapper. Bud shook his head, wondering why there would be trash out in this seemingly pristine wilderness, but he figured Shorty's camp was nearby and it had probably blown from there. He stuffed it into his shirt pocket and headed back to camp, wondering if Shorty was the only human out here like he'd said.

Once back, he asked Shorty where he kept his trash, showing him the wrapper.

"That's not from here," Shorty said with concern. "Bud, neither me nor Anderson eat Baby Ruths."

"It must've blown in from somewhere else," Bud replied. "Maybe some tourist threw it out their car window. It does look like it's seen better days."

Shorty replied, "Maybe, though the winds usually blow from here towards the highway, not the opposite. They come out of the north or west. But come on and have some breakfast. I made some pancakes and powdered eggs while you were up there. More coffee, too."

They sat in two foldable camp chairs Shorty brought from the tent, and Bud couldn't remember when food tasted so good. Shorty had some kind of berry jam they spread on the pancakes, and when Bud asked what it was, he replied, "I think it's huckleberry. Lily made it."

Over coffee, Bud finally asked, "Shorty, can you explain why you sent me a mining claim?"

Shorty laughed. "I was wondering when you'd ask. I was worried that the RCMP would put me in jail, and I wasn't sure what to do with it. See, Anderson sold it to me some time ago. He wanted to get rid of it. Some guy from Dawson wanted to buy it, and Anderson decided to go ahead and sell it to him, but then the guy came back and said he'd been bilked and wanted his money back. Anderson returned his money, and by then he just wanted to be done with it, so he sold it to me for a pittance."

"Why would the guy think he'd been bilked?" Bud asked.

"Well, have you ever heard of Cheechako Hill, over in Dawson?" Shorty asked.

Bud shook his head no, and Shorty continued. "Well, gold is 19 times heavier than water. That means it sinks and finds its way to the lowest part of the countryside, and that's the bottom of rivers and streams. Thus you get placer mining and gold panning, you bring up the gravel in the bottom of a stream and the gold will be there. One placer nugget found in 1898 weighed over 72 ounces, so most of the cheechakos went for panning, as they didn't have the wherewithal to actually mine. In 1904, the Klondike was the largest gold producer in Canada and the fourth largest in the world, and a lot of that was from placer claims. There was money to be made, though most went home broke, if they made it home at all."

Shorty paused to take a sip from his coffee mug, then continued.

"Anderson was a cracker jack geologist, and he knew about Cheechako Hill. Some smarty pants Stampeders decided to dig shafts right into the side of this hill near Dawson—to great derision—but lo and behold, they found gold—lots of it. They now call it Cheechako Hill."

"What, did they find a vein or something?" Bud asked.

"No, it was actually placer gold, of a sort. The hills overlooking the Klondike were lined with ancient stream beds that had long since ran dry and been uplifted by the Laramide Orogeny, the tectonic force that built these mountains. The Cheechakos who sank shafts in the hill stumbled upon a particularly rich stream bed of this gold and returned home fantastically wealthy. Anderson knew about these ancient stream beds, and his claim is a quartz claim, which means he has the rights to mine it. A lot of claims are just placer claims, just surface stuff. But the guy who bought it went and looked at it and had no clue what was going on and thought he'd been bilked."

"A little knowledge goes a long way, eh?" Bud replied.

Now Shorty leaned forward and said confidentially, "Bud, that claim I transferred to you has the potential to be very productive. I sometimes wonder *if* Anderson was killed, if it didn't have something to do with that claim."

"I have it in my pack," Bud said. "But you don't know who Anderson sold the claim to before you?"

"No, though I could probably find out if I went to the claims office. But another reason I sent it to you was an incentive for you to come up here. I know you well enough to know you're not greedy, but I thought maybe it would help whet your curiosity."

Now Bud was thoughtful. "Shorty, I think maybe that transferral was what made the Mounties think I knew where you were. Everything's electronic these days, and they were on the watch for anything to do with Jacob Doyle. When that transferral popped up in their database, it led them straight to me. Dougie McDougall seems like a sharp guy."

Shorty was quiet. "I should've thought of that," he said. "But

Dougie came all the way to Green River? Man, he really does want me in jail, doesn't he? I know Dougie pretty well. He's a good guy, though he can be overly serious, but I guess that's good if you're a Mountie. But Bud, I'm sure hoping nothing happens to get you into trouble. Maybe I didn't think this through very well."

Bud now replied, "And if they suspect you of also killing William, then that's one of them, and they get a bit more touchy about stuff like that. But no harm done with transferring the claim, as long as they don't catch up to me."

Bud sighed, then added, "And since I'm here illegally, they don't need a body to arrest me."

21

After breakfast, Bud and Shorty buttoned up camp and put everything away. The wind was really picking up, and they hoped it would soon die down and the day would warm up.

It was still chilly when they finally filled their daypacks with food and water and headed out, hiking along a long valley that appeared to go into the heart of the Tombstone Range.

The weather appeared to be getting worse the farther they went. The skies were now overcast and the clouds had an ominous blue tinge to them, which made Bud wary. The serrated ridges above them had disappeared in the mists.

"Do they have tornadoes up in this country?" Bud asked Shorty, who was ahead of him.

"Tornadoes?" Shorty asked. "I've never heard of one up here. But those clouds do look serious, don't they? I wish it would warm up."

They had started out following the creek, which Shorty had told Bud was called Wolf Creek, bushwhacking through a thick mosaic of willows interspersed with occasional white spruce, poplar, and aspen, startling birds and even what Shorty said was an Arctic squirrel.

As they continued on, they eventually left the creek, gradually gaining altitude, the going getting easier as the willows and trees were replaced by bushes and soft tundra. Most of the tundra plants had lost their autumn color, but Bud could tell they'd put on quite a show from the few that still had bright red and yellow leaves.

They now headed straight up a side slope, and once high enough, Bud could see a sharp scree-covered ridge ahead.

"Welcome to the Tombstones," Shorty said as they stopped to catch their breath. "The other side of this ridge is where Anderson died. We'll climb to the top where you can see the avalanche. If there weren't clouds, you'd have an awesome view of Tombstone Mountain that way and Mount Monolith over there."

He pointed, but Bud saw only gray clouds, which appeared to be moving in even faster.

"Then we'll be wanting to get the heck out of here," Shorty added. "Because it feels like snow."

Bud hoped the girls were on their way out, too. He then asked, "What were you guys doing up here?"

Shorty replied, "We were doing some geologic mapping for the government. The Tombstones are the southern part of the Ogilvie Mountains, which are near the Tintina Trench, which stretches from the Rocky Mountain Trench in British Columbia across the Yukon and into Alaska. It marks a collision point between the ancient North American continent and drifting fragments of other continents, called exotic terranes—exotic, because they came from other regions. Anyway, this area was mis-mapped by early geologists, and we were updating things a bit."

"Sounds really interesting," Bud said. "If you do make it back to Green River someday, I'd really enjoy going out with you and learning some geology."

Shorty replied, "The Colorado Plateau's really unique. Sometimes I really miss it. You know, Utah was also the edge of the ancient North American continent, just farther south from here. Some think the Colorado Plateau was actually a microplate, an exotic terrane that was accreted onto the continent. The Colorado Plateau is slowly rising, which partly accounts for all the interesting erosional features, all those big canyons and such. But let's get going—we'll be at the top of the slide here in a minute."

They soon reached the top of the ridge, where the winds almost took them off their feet. Hunkered down, Shorty pointed to a huge rockslide beneath their feet.

"The Tombstones are a volcanic extrusion, and you get these sharp loose igneous rocks on almost-vertical slopes. They're very treacherous. This is the one that caught Anderson. He's buried down there somewhere. I was over to the side more or I'd be there with him. We were both working that slope, taking rock samples. We knew it was unstable, but most everything out here is. Typically you get rock-slides in the early afternoon when things warm up—the frost between the layers melts and things slip, or maybe things will move in an earthquake, but this really isn't earthquake country. But after awhile, I moved over into the trees to take samples there and he was out of my view."

Bud now asked, "Is there any way you could prove you were at the bottom of the slope when it happened?"

"Not without an eye witness," Shorty said. "But let's get over here in the rocks out of the wind."

Now crouched behind an outcropping of large dark boulders, Bud asked, "How could they suspect you of causing the slide when you were down below with Anderson?"

Shorty shook his head. "The only way it would work is if I were lying. I looked for Anderson the remainder of that day and even stayed all night, sitting in the trees listening, in case he was injured and called out. Then I looked again all the next day. I finally found his hat, clear over in the trees a good 50 meters away. I figure it was blown off him by the avalanche wind. I hiked out and went to Dawson and contacted the Mounties. They came up here and searched, even had dogs, but found nothing. They took his hat. It was all I had left to remind me of him."

Bud replied, "But they must've found something to think you'd killed him. I mean, skiers and hikers get caught in avalanches and nobody suspects their buddies of murder."

Shorty replied, "They found something, but they wouldn't share what it was with me. I came back up here on top a couple of times but never saw anything out of the ordinary. But Bud, we need to get going back, but I'd like to hike down to the toe of the slide and look around one more time. I have a feeling this will be the last time I can get in here before next spring."

Bud nodded. "I understand. I'm kind of winded, as I'm not in as good of shape as you are, Shorty. I'd like to stay up here and look around some."

"I won't be gone long," Shorty said, heading down the edge of the slide, the wind making the going slow, trying to push him back upwards.

Bud carefully walked in front of the rock ledge above the avalanche. Finally, he could see where the dark volcanic rock was a lighter color—sure enough, it was where a boulder had come off and started the slide.

Now immediately under the fresh scar, he could see black marks nearby. The rock had definitely been blasted! Shorty had indeed heard the sound of a blast, though he'd undoubtedly also heard the sound of the large boulder cracking off and falling.

Bud took out his camera and took photos. Whoever blasted the rock not only had to know something about explosives, but they also had access to them. Was whoever set it off a hard-rock miner?

Putting his camera back in his pack, he began poking around to the side of the outcropping, knowing that whoever had blasted the boulder would've been a ways out from it.

He walked onto the tundra at the head of the slope, then began crisscrossing it, looking for any kind of clue that someone had been there. He'd once been a uranium miner, and even though it was different from gold mining, he knew a little about explosives and how far one needed to be back from the blast for safety.

Now wondering if the wind might have blown something on over to the back side of the ridge, he began searching the tundra there. About ready to concede defeat, he finally saw something partly sticking out of what looked to be a marmot hole.

Picking it up and brushing off the dirt, he could see it was a necklace. Hanging from a soft leather string were what appeared to be four huge bear claws, and Bud knew they had to be grizzly, as black bears didn't get that large. He carefully stuck it in his pack.

Bud now remembered that Lily had been wearing a necklace very similar, if not identical, to this. He'd asked her about it, and she'd told him she had shot a bear when it had tried to break into the roadhouse years ago, and she'd made necklaces from its claws, giving one to each of her kids and husband, and keeping one for herself. She had then recounted some of the many powerful connotations the grizzly had to the First Nations people.

He stood for a moment thinking—he now had three possible clues—whoever had set off the charge knew how to use explosives; they had access to such; and they were possibly related to Lily.

Now wondering when Shorty would return, Bud went back to the rock outcropping for shelter, as the wind was getting fiercer and fiercer. He looked down on the avalanche slope, wondering where Anderson was buried. Somehow, it seemed like an appropriate resting place for a geologist, especially with a name like Tombstone.

But suddenly, the peace and quiet were interrupted by what sounded like the crack of a nearby rifle shot.

Bud quickly ducked. Shorty was wrong, there were definitely others around.

22

Before Bud could even process what was happening, the ground beneath his feet was moving, taking him along with it. He somehow miraculously managed to quickstep his way to the side of the rock-slide, and thinking about it later, he knew it was only because he was at the very top where it hadn't gained much width or momentum.

The sound of thunder came from below, and soon a cloud of dust, caught by the wind, turned the air dark, practically choking him. He turned away and covered his mouth with his jacket sleeve.

He now knew the rifle shot was the sound of a large rock breaking loose. He'd heard that sound many times in the canyons near Green River, where rockfall was common, but he'd never been so close. It was one reason he never camped below cliffs.

The previous slide had apparently left things unstable enough that another rock had brought the rest of the slope down. He now wondered if Shorty was OK. It would be the greatest of ironies if he died on the same avalanche slope as Anderson had, Bud thought.

As the sound of the avalanche faded into the sound of the wind, Bud stood and carefully walked over to the edge of the ridge. The rock outcropping where he'd taken shelter was now completely gone, leaving nothing but a raw-looking cliff.

Wary of slipping, Bud leaned over and yelled, "Shorty! Shorty!" But he was sure there was no way anyone could hear, as the wind carried the sound away.

A thin cloud of dust was still rising from the slide below, and Bud could hear the occasional sound of rocks settling.

He sat down on a small hummock of tundra, not sure what to do. He could go down the edge of the slide and look for Shorty, but what if Shorty climbed the other side and they missed each other? If he had binoculars he could scan the slide for possible movement or any sign of Shorty, but if he'd been caught in the slide, there really wasn't much he could do.

He felt inept and incompetent, wanting to do something, but just sitting there. The clouds had now dropped down to where he was almost in them. It wouldn't be much longer, at the rate they were going, before it would be snowing, and he knew he could never find his way back alone.

Later, when it was all said and done, Bud could still feel the strangeness that went with what happened next, the pure unlikeliness and improbability of it all, and the thought always brought back the feeling of distance and filtered Arctic sunlight obscured by fog floating over dimly perceived mountains.

His phone rang.

He'd checked it numerous times, and it always showed no service. His battery was almost dead, and he'd intended to turn it off, but had forgotten. Shorty had told him they were far from any kind of tower, that people who needed to communicate used satellite phones in these parts. Bud had pretty much given up on ever calling out, and the last time he'd even charged it was at Joe's house the night he'd slept on their couch.

But there it was, his phone was ringing, and he could even make out the name on the caller ID—Howie McPherson.

"Yell-ow," Bud answered in amazement.

"Sheriff, is that really you?" Howie replied.

"It is, Howie, but I don't know how long we'll be connected. I think we're picking up some kind of skip."

Bud could already hear a weird garbling sound on the phone, followed by what sounded like some kind of Morse code.

"Is everything OK?" Howie asked.

"It's OK," Bud replied as the wind almost tore the phone from his hand.

"What?"

Now Bud could hear someone talking in a foreign language, tiny voices far far away. It reminded him of when he was a kid and his dad would make what he called DX, or long distance, calls on his HAM radio, calling places in lands Bud didn't even know existed, like the time they talked to a teacher in Peru.

"Howie, if you can hear me, I'm in the Yukon, near the Tombstone Mountains on Wolf Creek. We just had a rockslide, and it's starting to snow. I need to go. Is everyone there OK?"

Bud waited, but the signal had dropped, and he knew he'd lost him. He now wondered if anyone else had heard him describe where he was.

He shrugged. If so, good luck finding him in such an immense landscape. He'd turned off the GPS locator on his phone long ago when he'd arrived in Skagway.

It was now misting, and even though it wasn't that cold, the world had become gray, wet, and dreary, the mountains cloaked in low clouds and drifting fog, darkness beginning to settle in.

He could now hear someone coming along the ridge, and hoping it was Shorty, he called out, only to see several startled Dall sheep turn and run down the slope into the swirling fog.

Bud had heard stories about people getting lost in thick fog and walking in circles, and he had just decided that his best course of action was to go back to the rocks and try to find a sheltered place and wait out the storm, when he again heard something coming.

Soon, a headlamp shone in his direction.

"There you are," Shorty said casually, like a parent who'd just found their kid in the grocery store. He held up a GPS and said, "Let's go back."

23

"Better have some of this," Shorty said, handing Bud a small plastic container of peaches. "Lots of guys have died of scurvy up in these parts. In fact, Jack London was almost one of them. He was a Stampeder. He barely survived there in Dawson, some priest kept him from dying."

"No kidding?" Bud replied. "Actually, Shorty, I'm more worried about freezing to death than I am about scurvy."

They sat on the camp chairs in the wall tent, huddled around the small cook stove where Shorty was boiling water for hot tea, their dinner of canned stew now finished.

Bud continued, "Don't you think we'd be wise to get out of here and head back to the cafe?"

"No, we're better off here where we have shelter. The Dempster will be a muddy mess by now, and if we were to get a flat tire in this storm, it would be a pain fixing it. Besides, when it's this wet, it's easy to slide right off the road. Flat tires are common, as the gravel they used has a lot of sharp shale in it, and the road base is a slippery clay. We're better off driving after the road freezes up—it won't take long. Some of the coldest temperatures in Canada are here in the Tombstones. It's not uncommon to see minus 50°C here in the winter, which is pretty close to minus 60°F. Let's get rested up and head out in a few hours."

They now huddled in their chairs, drinking tea. After awhile, Bud said, "Shorty, I have a question for you. You said the last you saw, Anderson was out on the slope where the avalanche ran, then you went off a ways to the side where you couldn't see him. Would he have had time to hike up to the top before the avalanche hit?"

"Why would he do that?" Shorty asked, then said, "Oh, I get it. I see where you're going. I actually don't know. Maybe. But why would he set off an avalanche?"

"Maybe he was out to get you," Bud replied.

Shorty replied, "If he's still alive, where would he be? Nobody's seen him since the slide. It just doesn't make sense, Bud. I really don't think he would try to kill me. And I did find his hat down by the slide."

They both sat in silence, then Bud finally said, "Shorty, I got a phone call when I was up in the rocks from my deputy. At the time, I was pretty worried. I didn't know if you'd been in that second avalanche or not, and I wasn't sure I was going to make it out on my own in the dark and fog. I made the mistake of telling him where I was."

"I didn't know you had a GPS," Shorty replied.

"I don't," Bud said. "I just told him I was on Wolf Creek up in the Tombstones. I'm not even sure he heard me, as the phone went dead."

Shorty laughed. "And you're worried the Mounties were listening in? Even if they were, which is highly doubtful, especially with a skip, good luck finding someone with a vague description like that. But Bud, did you find anything up there worth mentioning?"

"I did. I found evidence someone had blasted the rocks. That first avalanche was no accident. I took photos."

Shorty was quiet for awhile, then asked, "What about the second one? It almost caught me."

"I didn't hear anything but a crack, the kind when a rock lets loose. No blast. I actually got caught in it for a second, and being that close, I would've heard it if it was blasted. I think it was just loose rocks that didn't quite go down with the first slide."

"Dang," Shorty said. "I'm glad you're OK. I would never forgive myself if I got you up here and something happened. But the Mounties must've found the blast marks like you did. Even if I did want to kill Anderson, I'm smarter than that. I would hide the evidence. One thing it does tell me is that whoever killed him knew a lot about mining explosives, enough to set off a charge, anyway. And they're not very thorough."

"Maybe they wanted people to know it was intentional," Bud replied. "But I'm wondering if they intended to kill you, also, Shorty. Or maybe you were the main target, and they got Anderson instead. Do you have any enemies?"

Shorty laughed. "Maybe a couple of my old university students who I failed. But no, not that I'm aware of. Maybe the guy Anderson sold the claim to was enough off his rocker to do something like that, though it doesn't seem very likely, especially since Anderson gave him his money back. The only thing I know is that sometimes it feels like I've got both good and bad guys looking for me."

"Good guys?" Bud asked.

"One day I feel like the Mounties are good guys, and the next, they're bad. I wish they would leave me alone. I want to go home. You know, Bud, I've done some things in the past that I'm not proud of, but it was never anything illegal. More like just being unkind to certain people, and at the time, I felt they deserved it."

Bud replied, "Well, my grandpa used to say that the past is like an old dime store novel. When you've got all you can get from it, you should throw it out and start a new one."

Shorty replied thoughtfully, "Most of the times I'm referring to have to do with people seeking me out to help them find gold. Just because I'm a geologist, they think I know where it is. If I do, why aren't I rich? Then they get mad because I won't help them. Human greed is hard to comprehend sometimes."

"Were any of them mad enough to want to kill you?"

Shorty paused, thinking, then said, "I don't think so. Killing someone usually goes beyond being mad, unless it's in the heat of the moment. This rockslide was premeditated, and things like that usually involve motives like revenge or money."

"True," Bud replied. "Ready for a second cup?"

He poured himself and Shorty both another cup of tea, then settled back in, his coat pulled tightly around him. If it got much colder, he would get his sleeping bag out and use it as a coat, he mused. The winds had died down some, but he could tell it was still snowing from the sound of snow sliding down the tent sides.

Bud now remembered the tiny rock he'd found on the tracks along Bennett Lake. He pulled out the small box of matches, hoping he hadn't lost it, then handed the small rock to Shorty.

"What does your geological expertise say this is?" Bud asked.

Shorty looked at it for a moment, then pulled out a small loupe from his pocket and held it up to the stove's light.

"I would swear it's a diamond," he replied. "If I had my old hand lens, I could tell for sure. I lost it somewhere, but it was a dandy, high powered and had good glass. Cassie got it for me when we were at Stanford for my birthday, even had my initials put on the handle."

"What, S.D.?" Bud asked.

"No, J.D. My real name is Jacob, you know. I was Professor Jacob Doyle, though I wasn't very well suited to being a prof. I hated the rules, and I wanted to be in the field."

"What kind of rules?" Bud asked.

"Well, one was you couldn't date your students, even though most of them were almost my age. Not that I cared, except for one..."

"Cassie?" Bud asked. "Not to get personal, Shorty, but she said you wanted her to come up here and work with you."

"I backed way off when I found out she was dating the guy she ended up marrying," Shorty replied.

"Did you know he died a few years ago?"

"No, I didn't know that. I'm sorry to hear it. What happened?"

"He was a rancher there in Green River and got killed in an equipment accident," Bud said.

Shorty was quiet for awhile, then said, "Well, that sure looks like a diamond. Where did you get it?"

"On the tracks along Lake Bennet, not far from Pennington Station."

Shorty replied, "That's odd. I'll have to think about that one." He then asked, "You ever heard of George Carmack?"

"No, but we came through a little town called Carmacks on our way up here," Bud replied.

"It's named for George. He was one of the first to discover gold here, which started the gold rush. He was from the States and came up here and married a Tagish woman named Shaaw Tlaa, or Kate. Lily and her family are Tagish, you know."

Bud thought of the bear-claw necklace in his pack. He'd decided not to mention it until he could find out more about it.

Shorty sipped his hot tea, then continued. "Anyway, George was up in this country with his wife, her brother Keish, also called Skookum Jim, their nephew Kaa Goox, or Dawson Charlie, and Tagish Charlie, her uncle. One night, in 1896, George Carmack had a dream. He'd been having a feeling that something amazing was about to happen, and he dreamed about two huge salmon with gold-plated scales and twenty-dollar gold pieces for eyes. Now, instead of interpreting the dream as a sign he was near gold, he decided that the dream meant the fishing would be good. I don't think he had a greedy bone in his body, because even after they found a piece of solid gold as large as his thumb in the nearby bedrock, he seemed more interested in fishing. But they staked a claim there on Rabbit Creek, and it later became known as Bonanza Creek, the center of the gold rush. I always thought it was interesting that the fellow who helped start the rush wasn't even that interested in gold."

Bud was quiet, thinking of what Shorty had said. He thought of the tens of thousands of Stampeders and how some must've pined for home, many of them doomed to never return. He wondered if he would end up like the ones who never made it back.

Now a voice from outside the tent said, "That's a pretty good story, if it's true, but you forget to mention that Carmack was called Lyin' George. Can I come in? I'm freezing to death out here."

"Come on in, Dougie," Shorty said, looking both surprised and pained. "And tell us what you're doing out here."

24

"How'd you come to be in these parts in a blizzard?" Shorty asked the Mountie, who was now seated on a cot. "Are you trying to replay the saga of the Lost Patrol?"

Dougie, lit up by Shorty's headlamp, was wearing an impressive blue down coat with the Mountie insignia on its shoulders.

He replied, "I hope not. And I hope you don't consider that a humorous thing to say to a Mountie."

Shorty looked at Bud. "The Lost Patrol was a group of four Mounties who went missing in these parts in 1910, though back then, they were called the Royal Northwest Mounted Police. They were going from Fort McPherson, Northwest Territories, to Dawson City, approximately 620 miles, on foot and by dogsled, to deliver mail and dispatches. They lost their way and died from cold and starvation."

Shorty now looked directly at Dougie, saying, "And no, Dougie, I was simply remarking on your unexpected presence in an unexpected place and time in unexpected weather. Let me make you some hot tea."

Shorty now lit the small cookstove and put water on to boil, the light now casting shadows and immediately warming up the tent.

Soon handing Dougie a cup of tea, Shorty asked, "What exactly can we do for you, Sergeant?"

"Your clutch-popping trick almost lost us," Dougie said dryly.

"Still no body, eh?" Shorty asked. "And no, I don't find that humorous, either. Luke Anderson was my friend."

"I really don't need a body to arrest you, Jacob," Dougie said.

Bud sensed a tension between them, and he wondered if it went beyond Anderson's death. He also wondered if Dougie had heard them talking about the diamond he'd found.

"I'm not trying to make light of things, Dougie, but saying you don't need a body to arrest me really is a pretty funny statement," Shorty said, grinning in the dim light of the stove, which he'd left on so as to warm things up.

Dougie nodded his head patiently as if used to Shorty's sense of humor, then added, "It'll come when the time's right. But why don't you introduce me to your colleague?"

Shorty looked at Dougie in surprise, then said, "You don't need any introduction. He's an old friend of yours."

Dougie said, "I'm sorry, but I don't quite recognize him." He then looked directly at Bud and said, "My apologies, sir. There's not much light in here."

"No problem," Bud said congenially. "Bud Shumway."

Dougie's eyes grew big, and Bud could tell he was totally flummoxed. Finally, Dougie said, "Here in Canada?"

Bud nodded, holding his hands to the stove's small flame.

"How did you get here? Last we could tell, you were on a plane to Whitehorse, but never got off there, though your luggage did."

"It wasn't a big deal," Bud said. "I just went with the flow."

"I suspected you knew where Jacob was," Dougie said.

"I actually didn't," Bud replied. "I hadn't seen him for 30 years."

"Then how did you know to come here?"

"Like I said, I went with the flow," Bud said. "It's amazing where life will take you sometimes."

Dougie looked suspicious, then said, "You didn't go through any of the border patrols. How did you get into Canada?"

"Well," Bud replied. "Basically, I walked in on the railroad tracks along Bennett Lake, but I didn't know I was entering illegally."

"That's somewhat impressive," Dougie said.

"He's so good he's even on the Internet," Shorty added, half-kidding.

Bud then said, "I know I'm here illegally, whether intentional or not. You can arrest me and I'll go quietly—I'm not armed. But what good would that do? I really believe Shorty here is innocent, and I already have some ideas about what happened. In honor of your fellow Mountie, William Walker, you should let me help you solve this. Arresting me would just be a waste of resources."

Dougie sat for some time in the soft light of the stove, and it seemed like the snow had stopped, for Bud could no longer hear it sliding down the sides of the tent.

Shorty also sat quietly, then said, "Dougie, I taught Bud in high school. I hadn't seen him since. But we have a mutual acquaintance who put me in touch with him when I realized he was maybe someone who could help prove my innocence. He truly didn't know who you were talking about there in his office, because he always knew me as Shorty Doyle, not Jacob. Nobody in Green River called me Jacob. You can arrest us both, but I think you'd be better off doing your duty as a lawman to let us help you solve this, or at least let Bud. He's an LEO, just like you. You won't find anyone who's more of a straight shooter."

"A straight shooter?"

"That's what they call someone in the States who's honest and straightforward."

"Oh. Well, right now, I wouldn't know what to do with him anyway. If I arrested him, I'd have to take him to Whitehorse, and I can't do that. I'm here to enlist your help, not arrest anyone."

"Our help?" Bud asked with surprise.

"Yes. We have a group of eleven girls and two adults who are late coming back from a camping trip in Tombstone Territorial Park. They were supposed to come out yesterday. We're gathering a search party. Jacob knows this country like no one else. I've come to ask his help, and yours too, Mr. Shumway, should you wish to use your talents in this manner. I'm sure as a trained LEO in the States, you have experience with search and rescue?"

"I do," Bud said simply. "I would be glad to help in any way possible."

"Sign me up, too," Shorty added. "I do know the country—like the back of my hand."

25

Bud rode in the passenger seat of Dougie's RCMP Range Rover, his feet pushed as far up against the heater as possible. Far enough behind so as to not get showered in their mud came Shorty in his old Ford, and just as Shorty had predicted, the Dempster Highway was a mess, though gradually freezing.

"You have to travel this road carefully in the dark," Dougie said. "Because there's usually no shoulder and sometimes it's quite a good distance down. The maintenance crews keep busy, as do the tow trucks from Dawson. In fact, there's a highway maintenance camp not too far ahead."

"A camp? Do people live there?"

"Only in the summer. It's too far to drive here every day for work, especially when working farther up the highway. There are several camps along the Dempster."

They drove on, and Bud was glad it had stopped snowing. The fog was now heavy enough that, combined with a waxing moon, it made the landscape seem eerie and strange.

Finally, trying to make conversation to stay awake, Bud asked, "Is it true you Mounties always get your man?"

Dougie laughed. "That came from Hollywood. Our actual motto is *Maintiens le droit.*"

"What does that mean?"

"It's French for *Maintaining the Right*, or *Defending the Law*."

"Why French?" Bud asked.

"Everything in Canada is bilingual, French-English, by law. I'm sure you noticed all the signs are in both."

"I did," Bud replied. "It seems like it would kind of double the cost of everything. But does everyone in Canada speak French?"

"Out here in the western parts, most people speak only English, though they may be able to read a little French. But back in Quebec, there are people who speak only French but can only read a little English."

"So, your bilingual signs are unifying the country," Bud joked.

"One could hope," Dougie said. "But I don't think Quebec will ever be happy being a part of Canada, and lots of people wish they would separate. But heck, not even 'Berta and B.C. can seem to get along. People are just naturally contentious, is my belief. Like that old woman who called you when I was in your office about whatever it was, making your deputy come out and explain things."

"Mrs. Jensen?" Bud laughed. "At least when she's not keeping us busy she's baking us cookies."

"We get some interesting calls, too," Dougie replied. "Actually, I got appraised of one on my way out here from Dawson. Dispatch said someone was very concerned because their friend was somewhere in the Yukon being chased by wolves in a rockslide near a tombstone. Dispatch said it came from way down in the States. Now what would someone expect us to do with information like that?"

"You did quite well, considering," Bud grinned. "You found the person they were worried about. But you forgot to call them back."

"What?" Dougie asked incredulously. "I found them?"

Bud laughed. "The world works in strange ways, Dougie. I got a skip call way up in the Tombstones when I was with Shorty. It was from my deputy, you remember him, Howard McPherson. I haven't been in contact with anyone back home, and he was worried. The call dropped right after I told him I was in the Yukon, near the Tombstone Mountains on Wolf Creek near a rockslide—almost verbatim. I'd wondered if he heard any of it."

Dougie shook his head. "That's one for the books."

They rode on, the wheels crunching the freezing gravel, making the road sound even more treacherous than it was.

Finally, Bud said, "You know, when I was a kid, we had shows down in the States like *Sergeant Preston of the Yukon*, and I read every book I could find about what the early maps called the Great Northern Mystery. I didn't come from a well-travelled family—we never had the money—but I've always had a wanderlust to come up here. I never dreamed it would be like this, riding with a Mountie along a remote highway in Yukon Territory in the fog on a SAR mission."

"Life can take us for a ride sometimes," Dougie replied. "I felt the same way when I was down in your part of the States. It's such a different landscape from up here, and I really hope to get back down there someday."

"Well, if you do," Bud said, "Look me up, and I'll show you the country—assuming I'm not in a Canadian jail, that is. Believe me, I don't take illegal entering lightly."

"We don't either," Dougie said, glancing at Bud. "Maybe you could explain exactly how you pulled that off. Our border patrol takes a great deal of pride in their effectiveness, and you threw us for a loop. We thought we had a good handle on your whereabouts until you disappeared on the way to Whitehorse."

"I was amazed at how quickly you got a Mountie on my plane and even got her a seat next to me," Bud replied.

Dougie looked surprised. "A Mountie on the plane with you?"

"I didn't get her name. She said she lived in Dawson. An older woman, well dressed. Said she was a Mountie."

Dougie looked incredulous. "That was likely Sergeant Major Sue Hazelton. She's my supervisor and our official photographer, does a lot of forensics. She just got back from a conference down in Denver. She sat right next to you? Unbelievable."

Bud laughed. "I thought you guys were pretty sharp to be able to track me like that, especially that quickly."

"I found out from your wife where you were going, and we contacted the airlines, but that was the extent of our tracking you. Once you were supposed to arrive in Whitehorse and didn't, we knew we'd lost you. I was going to drive back in my rental and enjoy the countryside, but I ended up flying just to try and catch up with you."

"My own wife told you where I was," Bud said in mock bitterness.

"She sure has a nice B&B," Dougie said. "But why not tell me the details of how you got up here?"

Bud explained every step of his journey to Dougie as they drove slowly along the Dempster. Finally, finished with his story, he asked, "Exactly where are we going?"

Dougie replied, "You sure seem to have a way of landing on your feet. But I wish I knew where we were going. All I know is the lodge where the girls were supposed to be staying last night called us and said they were overdue and had told them they were camping in the Tombstones. We have no idea exactly where. I can't get ahold of anyone in Whitehorse who knows, either. So we're going to meet at the park's interpretive center and take it from there, assuming their van is parked there. I have people coming from the Dawson and Carmacks detachments and can call in more if needed, but it's going to be slow going until daylight. We usually wouldn't even risk it and come out like this in a storm at night, but these are kids we're talking about."

Bud nodded his head. "I would do the same," he said, then added, "Well, actually, I *am* doing the same. But Dougie, I know where they went."

Bud could see Dougie turn in surprise towards him as he added, "They told me they were going to camp at Grizzly Lake."

"We're almost at the Grizzly Ridge trailhead," Dougie added. "That goes to the lake. We'll stop there. I'll let the others know."

As Dougie reached for his radio, he said, "Here legally or not, Bud, welcome to Canada. Let's hope your presence has just helped save some lives."

26

"We probably would've driven right past this in the dark," Dougie said, nodding towards the white van parked near the highway. "Maybe we'd have seen it in daylight, but not tonight with this fog. We would've been on a wild goose chase if we hadn't known where to look."

Bud got out and tried to open the doors of the van, but they were all locked. He looked for a note or anything that might signal a change of plans, but found nothing.

By the time everyone had arrived and Dougie had debriefed them, Bud was wet and chilled, the coat he'd bought at Canadian Tire obviously not up to the task—even though it had red maple leaves on the shoulders, which was partly why he'd bought it.

Dougie handed him a GPS, and noting his coat was soaked, went to the back of his Range Rover and pulled out a coat like the one he was wearing.

"Here, put this on," he said, handing Bud the coat. "It's Gore Tex and down and will keep you nice and dry."

Bud took off his coat, putting on the new one, then, noting the Mountie insignias on the arms, asked, "Are you sure I won't get arrested for impersonating an RCMP officer?"

Dougie smiled. "With your luck, you'd probably get promoted to Commissioner."

Shorty, who had come up behind them, said, "Nice coat, Bud. And Dougie, when you finally figure out I'm innocent, you can get me one of these to show you're sorry. The blue is nice, but no insignias, please."

Dougie, who now looked irritated, looked even more so when Shorty seemed to take over his role as commanding officer and began rounding everyone up.

As far as Bud could tell, the SAR team consisted of about eight men and women, all dressed for winter and carrying packs that he knew contained not only survival gear, but medical supplies, which he hoped they wouldn't need. A couple had collapsable litters strapped to their backs.

Shorty now said. "OK, everyone, here's the low-down on this trail. I know some of you, heck, maybe all of you, have hiked it before, since it's a popular route into the Tombstones, but for those who haven't, like Officer Shumway here, I'll give you a quick overview."

He paused and looked around as the fog began to lift, then continued. "It looks like we may get lucky and have this dang fog go away. Anyway, it's about 10 klicks to Grizzly Lake, which doesn't sound far, but it crosses steep rocky slopes after you leave the trees. Be careful to stay to the left on Grizzly Creek when you meet Cairnes Creek."

He paused, then said, "The real test will be when we get to the lake and see if they're there or not. You have to try to get lost up here, as you have to climb out of the creek's drainage, but people have done it, as I would guess you all well know. If the kids aren't at the lake, we'll reconnoiter there. By then it should be dawn and we can see where we're going. Back to you, Sergeant McDougald."

Dougie, still looking irritated, said, "Grizzly Lake is an overnight trip, and normally pre-booking is required, but since the interpretive center is now closed for the season, we don't know if this is really where they went or not. We're going on what Mr. Shumway here was told by one of the group leaders, as well as their vehicle being parked at the trailhead, so it's very likely they're up here somewhere. Also, even though it's late in the season, note the trail's name and always be bear aware. OK, we're off."

The hike started relatively easy, the trail following the creek through the boreal forest, and though he was in the rear, Bud was careful to not get behind, even though he was tired. Everyone had their headlamps on, and where the fog had cleared, moonshadows filtered through the forest of black poplar, giving everything a mysterious air.

Everyone was silent, hoping to hear the sound of talking or even calls for help—anything that would point them to the missing group, which was supposed to have been down in Dawson by early afternoon the previous day.

They trudged on for some time, eventually coming to where Cairnes Creek met Grizzly Creek, staying to the left as Shorty had told them. As they continued on, Bud could soon make out steep slopes on either side in the moonlight, and the effect was surreal, unlike anything he'd ever seen, the lifting fog making the wet volcanic rock look like black shiny obsidian. The jagged peaks and dark landscape reminded Bud of something from a dream, it all seemed so unreal.

The group now stopped for a break, drinking hot tea from thermoses as the moon set across the ragged top of the Tombstones.

Now Dougie held up his hand for all to be quiet.

"Listen," he commanded. "I thought I heard something."

Standing there in the deep Yukon wilds, Bud now heard a sound he'd never heard before. The cries of a pack of wolves floated through the cold sub-Arctic air, a sound that some have described as lonely, but that Bud felt was more like a happy celebration—maybe of the end of the storm, or perhaps at having just killed dinner, or maybe just at being alive. It left him feeling a bit frightened, yet in awe.

He could tell that, even though the group was seasoned Northerners, the sound had the same effect on them, as everyone stood quietly.

"Will they harm the kids?" Bud finally asked a woman standing nearby.

"It's extremely rare for a wolf to harm a human," she replied. "But let's hope the kids are sticking together. Who knows what might befall one out alone, but mountain lions are much more of a risk than anything else."

Bud was familiar with lions, as they were about the only large predator in the canyons back home. Even at that, it was rare to ever see one, and some called them the ghosts of the forests. But hearing the wolves made him uncomfortable, even though he found them fascinating.

Shorty was leading the group, and Dougie had been close behind him, but he now fell back next to Bud.

"The fog's gone, Bud. Have you ever seen anything like that?" Dougie pointed upwards, and Bud gasped. There, above them, was an undulating belt of crimsons and greens across a sky studded with more stars than Bud had ever imagined could exist. The lights were so low they looked like they would get caught in the precipitous spires surrounding Bud and Dougie, and Bud was surprised at how fast the colors moved and changed in the sky, shimmering with a rare magic.

He was finally seeing the aurora, and he knew that the red was the rarest of all colors, as it was caused when electrons strike oxygen atoms at higher altitudes, which happened only during intense solar activity. The long curtain stretched across the sky, moving as if alive, the colors fading, then growing intense again.

Before he could help himself, Bud had taken out his camera, and setting it on a nearby rock to stabilize it, was taking photos.

"I know we need to catch up, but one quick favor, Dougie. Would you take a picture of me backlit by the aurora? This may be a once in a lifetime thing for me."

Dougie framed Bud in the viewfinder and took several shots, then Bud studied the results on the LED screen.

"Perfect," he said happily. "Just enough light to see me in the glow. Let's hurry and catch up."

Later, when back in Green River, Bud had the photo enlarged and framed, hanging it above his recliner in the bungalow. It had an otherworldly quality to it—black volcanic spires in the background and his hair glowing a reddish pink from the light of what looked like a giant red curtain behind him, the RCMP insignias on the coat clearly visible almost as if lit from within.

Now Dougie again held up his hand, signaling for Bud to be quiet.

After a moment, Bud said, "I hear it, too, Dougie. It's coming from up there."

He pointed to what looked like a sharp ridge directly above them glowing in the red light, a small patch of snow below it.

Dougie replied, "What do you think that sound is? We need to catch up to the group, but I feel like we'd be negligent if we didn't go check."

"I agree," Bud said. "We have to go look."

They both slowly worked their way up the steep slope beneath what Bud thought looked like a volcanic dike, like the spine of some huge black dragon. It was slow going, and they both had to stop and catch their breath often.

Now, finally standing next to the patch of snow, Bud shivered at what his headlamp revealed.

He said, "Look at this, Dougie, here in the snow. Blood. Lots of blood. And it's not from the glow of the aurora, it's the real deal."

27

Dougie examined the snow carefully in his headlamp, then said, "Bud, this isn't blood. It's what we call watermelon snow. It's found at high elevations and is a cold-loving algae that lives on the snow. It has a red pigment that dyes the surrounding area, giving the effect of a pink or red snow field."

Relieved, they both stood at the base of the dike, but could now hear nothing. Wondering if it had been an owl or some other night creature, they both quietly shone their lights around the huge dike looming above.

And after it was all said and done, when Bud described that night to others, he called it "the night of many wonders." After seeing the volcanic rocks glow in the moonlight, hearing wolves, seeing the aurora, and finding watermelon snow for the first time, each a marvel in their own right, he was still unprepared for what he saw next.

As he shone his light on the black dike, it caught a momentary reflection of what looked to be a thousand tiny lights. He thought for a moment it was some kind of mica or quartz, but pointing his light back that way again, he could see that part of the dike seemed to glow with tiny points of light, as if set with diamonds.

"Do you see that?" Bud asked Dougie, who nodded his head in

amazement.

Now suddenly, they could hear the sound again, and it was clearly someone or something moaning. Careful to not slip or knock down rocks and start a slide on the steep slope, they worked their way to its source, which seemed to be the same place as the points of light.

Once there, Bud could make out something lighter-colored in the rocks, and when they both shone their lights on it, they could see it was a woman, all crumpled into a mass on the ground. Their head-lamps picked up the tiny points, reminding Bud of the tiny garden lights Wilma Jean had strung around the front porch of her B&B back home.

Now the woman spoke softly.

"I know you're here to take me to Heaven. Can we go now? I'm cold."

Bud bent down closer to where he could see her face.

It was Jan, the girls' hockey team leader!

He took off his glove and put his hand on her forehead, saying, "Since I'm not sure they would let me in, hows about Dawson instead? I think it might also be a tad closer."

The woman, confused, said, "I'm not sure I want to spend eternity in Dawson."

"From what I've heard," Bud replied, "You're right. You might like Whitehorse better. But Jan, it's Bud Shumway. I have the RCMP with me. We're going to get you back home."

She looked cold and disheveled.

"Bud? You mean the Bud in the van? With Lindie?"

Bud was examining her as she spoke, trying to get an idea of how seriously she was injured, as Dougie now shone his headlamp on her.

"Jan, how long have you been sitting here? Do you remember?" Bud asked.

"A long time," she replied. "I'm so cold."

Bud now took her hand, which felt like ice. She was shivering, and he knew she was hypothermic. They needed to get her warmed up fast, but there was nothing nearby, no wood for a fire—nothing but rocks.

"Jan, can you stand up?" He asked. "Let's try it. Is your ankle hurt?" He stood and tried to gently pull her up towards him.

She moaned and went limp, then started sobbing.

"I just want to go to sleep. Let me take a little nap, then we'll try again."

Bud was now examining her ankle, which was swollen and bruised.

"Jan, I'm going to push on your ankle here a little and it's going to hurt a bit. I need to find out if it's broken or not."

He gently pressed, but felt nothing that felt like broken bone. She had no reaction at all, which surprised him until he realized she was so cold she probably felt nothing.

"OK, I think you just have a badly twisted ankle," he said gently, trying to reassure her. "If we can get out of here, we can go home and drink lots of hot tea and get warmed up. Let's try standing again. Do your best. Dougie, this is one of the group leaders."

Dougie now took off his pack, pulling out a thermos, pouring its contents into the lid.

"Jan, I'm Sergeant McDougald. Drink this tea. It will warm you up."

Dougie held the cup to her lips as she drank.

"No wonder she's so cold," Bud said. "She's soaking wet from the fog."

Bud took off his coat and carefully put it on her, saying, "Dougie, let's get her back to your vehicle. She needs more than what we can give her out here, like a warm heater and maybe even a hospital."

"Now *you'll* get hypothermic," Dougie protested.

"Not if we keep moving. We're going to have to pretty much carry her back, but if we can get her to go under her own power even somewhat, it will help warm her up."

One on each side, Bud and Dougie carefully carried Jan down off the steep slope using their arms as a makeshift sling, and once back on the trail, managed to get her to hop along between them, hoping it would help warm her up.

Jan had finally quit shivering, but Bud knew time was of the essence. They needed to get her warmed up, plus he was starting to get cold himself.

He was surprised at how quickly they made it back to the vehicles. They buckled Jan into the front seat of the Rover where she would be next to the heater, Dougie taking off the Mountie coat and wrapping her in a wool blanket from head to toe. Bud retrieved his old coat from the back seat.

"I've got it covered, Bud," Dougie said. "I'll radio out for an ambulance to meet me. I think you should stay. We need to get word to the SAR team that we found one of the leaders."

Bud was somewhat disappointed, though he knew Dougie was right. He was exhausted and hungry and looking forward to seeing Lindie at the Klondike Cafe and drinking hot tea with Lily.

He grabbed his pack, saying, "Sounds good. I'll hang out here for awhile and get rested, then head back up."

Turning back, he could now see the upper ramparts of the Tombstone Range lit with the early rays of dawn. It was a spectacular sight, one Bud knew he would probably never see again, with the huge square top of Mount Monolith beginning to glow, the last tendrils of fog drifting across its face.

As he pulled out his camera, Dougie handed him the Mountie coat.

Bud looked puzzled, but Dougie just said, "Bud, keep it. You need it. It's a gift from the RCMP for your help."

Bud took the coat and put it back on, now remembering the rock sample in its pocket, which he'd managed to grab while up under the big volcanic dike.

And as Dougie and Jan headed back down the Dempster Highway, he turned his attention back to the red glow on the top of Monolith, framing it and the golden fog clouds perfectly with his camera, knowing the light would soon change.

It was a photo that would later earn him a purple grand-champion ribbon back home at the Carbon County Fair, even though Wilma Jean declined to put it in her "Best of Bud" calendar for that year, saying it made her feel cold and lonely.

28

"Sleepin' on the job, eh?"

A voice woke Bud, who had tried his best to stay awake, but had finally crawled into Shorty's Ford and dozed off. He hadn't been surprised to find the Ford unlocked, as he and Shorty were from the same background, from a culture where people left things unlocked in case of emergencies like this one. It was all part of the Code of the West.

Bud jerked awake. Had the SAR folks made it back?

Standing next to the Ford was a scruffy looking fellow who looked like he'd slept in his clothes, though Bud wasn't one to judge, having done the same, though the truth was he hadn't been doing much sleeping lately.

"Mornin'," Bud said, now getting out of the Ford, noting that the fellow wasn't one of the SAR group. It was a beautiful sunny morning, all traces of fog gone, though a dampness still lingered in the air. Bud noted the fellow didn't have a coat, but was instead wearing a heavy sweater with holes in the elbows.

The guy now seemed nervous. Bud saw him quickly stick something in his pocket that looked like it could be a screwdriver.

"Sorry, Inspector, I sure didn't mean to wake you."

"It's OK," Bud replied. "I need to get around anyway. Are you looking for someone?"

"Oh, no, no sir, I just stopped thinkin' you all might need help, that maybe somethin' important was goin' on, with all the Mountie cars around."

The fellow appeared to be getting more nervous by the minute, and Bud realized he must think he was a Mountie, since he was wearing the Mountie coat.

"Are you camping out here?" Bud asked.

"No, I was just passin' through on my way to Eagle Plains. Thought I'd stop and check up on everyone."

Bud's intuition told him the man was probably lying. Was he thinking to stop and see what he could steal and had found Bud instead? Why had he woke him instead of slipping away? Bud was quiet, saying nothing.

The silence appeared to make the man even more nervous, and he pulled something from his pocket and handed it to Bud.

"Here, have one of these. Gets the energy goin'." He handed Bud a small Baby Ruth candy bar.

"Thanks, but do you have some for yourself?" Bud asked, opening it and carefully putting the wrapper in his coat pocket.

"I do," the man replied, pulling out another and opening it, acting for a moment as if he was going to toss the wrapper, then instead sticking it in his pocket.

They stood for a moment, both munching, then Bud said. "You look like you could use a coat. I have one you can have."

He pulled the Canadian Tire coat from the Ford and handed it to the man, saying, "I'm not really a Mountie. They gave me the coat for helping them. There's a search and rescue going on, some kids are missing. Did you happen to see anyone? A bunch of girls and a woman."

The man took the coat, looking surprised, and slipped it on. He admired the red maple leaves on the shoulders for a moment, holding out his arms and feeling the fabric, even though it was a bit too big for him.

"This is really nice of you. No, I haven't seen anyone, besides you, that is. Sorry to wake you, but I thought maybe you were sick or somethin', out here like this."

"I'm Bud Shumway," Bud offered the man his hand.

"Grady Johnson."

Bud had wondered if he wasn't talking to Grady, based on the description Lily had given him back at the cafe. Grady's demeanor now changed, and he seemed to relax. He pulled something from the coat pocket and handed it to Bud.

"Did you forget this?"

It was Bud's harmonica!

"Thanks. I'm not sure I could live without this," Bud joked.

"I can play it," Grady said, reminding Bud of a little kid. Bud handed him the harmonica, saying, "I could sure use a lesson or two."

Grady started playing a blues tune, and though Bud wasn't sure what it was called, he thought it was maybe something from Bo Diddly. Bud was amazed at how good he was.

"You sound like you could play professionally," Bud said in admiration.

"I used to play with a band up in Whitehorse," Grady replied. "We called ourselves the Midnight Pucks. You know, Midnight Sun plus hockey pucks."

Bud grinned. "Sounds like fun."

"Yeah, we had a lot of fun, even got paid once in awhile. Here, let me show you some tricks."

Bud and Grady now sat leaning against the Ford's tires, Grady giving Bud an impromptu harmonica lesson, the business of the day taking back seat to a carpe diem moment.

Before long, Bud had learned the difference between a riff and a lick (Grady told him that licks tend to be shorter), and had even learned how to play a couple of each type, including one used by Little Pete, who played with Muddy Waters.

And as Bud tried to adapt the licks and riffs he'd learned to the few songs he knew, he felt that maybe this harmonica thing was within his grasp after all. He could even see maybe jamming some with Howie and his band when he got back home.

Finally, Grady stopped, saying, "I need to get going."

They both stood, and Bud thanked him for the lesson, then said, "Why don't you play in a band anymore, Grady?"

"That was back before the government ruined everything," Grady replied, spitting on the ground in disgust.

"Lily told me how they shut down the Klondike Cafe," Bud replied.

Grady looked surprised. "You know Lily? She and Stan were sure good to me, though I didn't repay the favor. She may not know it, but I quit drinkin' after I left their place. I'm tryin' to put myself back together, but I need to get over this anger. I'm homeless now, you know, and it's all because of that damn government geologist."

Bud knew Grady was referring to the guy who'd told Lily and Stan they had to upgrade their septic system.

"He was a geologist?"

"Yeah, a geologist. If I can figure out where he disappeared to, he's toast," Grady replied.

Bud was speechless.

He could now hear someone coming down the trail, and before he could say sic 'em, Grady had handed Bud the harmonica and was gone, jumping into an old Willys Jeep pickup and heading back towards Dawson and the Klondike Cafe, going the opposite direction of Eagle Plains.

It was then that Bud could hear Shorty's voice ringing out, accompanied by what sounded like an entire chorus of girls:

> The ants go marching one by one, hurrah, hurrah,
> The ants go marching one by one, hurrah, hurrah!

To Bud, it was one of the most moving songs he'd ever heard, and he couldn't help but tear up a little.

29

It was late afternoon when Bud woke, and it took him awhile to figure out he was in the Klondike Cafe, as he was the only one there in the quiet. Lindie was dutifully curled up by his backpacking pad, happily wagging her tail when he got up and gave her a Barkie Biscuit.

"Where is everyone?" He asked as she ate the biscuit, scattering pieces everywhere.

"You better get it all, or Lily will be after us," Bud said, tapping his toe by the crumbs, which she quickly grabbed up.

It seemed lately that Bud's life was a series of sleep-deprived stretches interspersed with a few hours of sleep here and there, none of it having any rhyme or reason. He couldn't remember when he'd actually had a good night's rest, but he thought it was back on Joe's couch, and he'd lost track of the days since.

The SAR group had found the girls still camped by Grizzly Lake, waiting for Jan to return from what was supposed to be a short hike up the ridge to take photos of the group camped below.

She'd mysteriously disappeared when the fog had come in, and Carolyn had wisely ordered everyone to stay put, as she knew a rescue party would show up sooner or later, and she hoped Jan would find her way back eventually. As it was, everyone was fine, though somewhat shaken. Bud had assured them that Jan would be OK, though her ankle would take some time to heal.

He'd ridden back to the cafe with Shorty to find Stan there with the supplies from Whitehorse, which Shorty had then decided to take on back to camp. Shorty seemed determined to finish his geological survey before winter hit, saying he was almost done.

Bud had declined to accompany him, knowing he was on his last legs if he didn't get some rest, and since Dougie now knew where the camp was, it all seemed somewhat moot anyway.

Bud put the teapot on the stove, then sat and drank a cup, which immediately made him feel better. He noticed Lily now had a jar of honey, probably something Stan had brought back from Whitehorse, Bud figured.

As he sat there, he thought about the tension he'd noticed between Shorty and Dougie. He now suspected that it had something to do with a difference in their interpretation of the law—and probably of life in general. Given what he'd now observed about them, he figured Shorty was more concerned with the intent of the law, while Dougie was more of a letter of the law kind of guy. It made sense that they would clash.

He himself felt that laws were made for helping people stay civilized, not to blindly turn people into law-breakers. He and Shorty were more on the same side of the fence in that respect, both believing that there could be extenuating circumstances.

And yet, Dougie had given him the Mountie coat, which Bud suspected was a straightforward violation of the rules, so he wasn't totally rule bound, if one wanted to call it that. But he did know from experience that people who strictly followed the rules were typically irritated by people like Shorty. Bud also knew that working in what geologists called deep time gave one a different perspective on things, making day by day things seem less important.

The tea gone, Bud pulled a bag of fruit and nuts from his pack, then decided to take Lindie for a walk before the sun set. He wanted to go into Dawson and get a room, call Wilma Jean, take a hot shower, and sleep some more, but he didn't want to leave Lindie at the cafe alone, since everyone was gone. He thought about taking her, but in spite of Joe giving him the dog, he wondered if she really was Joe's to give, and he didn't want to make Lily unhappy.

He grabbed Lindie's leash and put on his Mountie coat, then went out the back door. A path wound down to the river through the willows, and Lindie followed him. They startled two gray jays similar to a pair that Lily had pointed out the afternoon he'd spent at the cafe.

Lily read a lot, since there wasn't much else to do, and Bud had noted a nice stack of books there at the cafe, most from the Dawson library. She had books on birds and flowers and even geology, plus a few mystery novels. He'd started one that was set down in Utah but had given up on it, as it seemed that all the protagonist wanted to do was sit around drinking coffee with dollops of ice cream in it, and besides, it made him miss home.

One of the books Lily had was about Klondike geology and talked about the most recent glaciation in the area some 12,000 years ago, when a glacier flowed down the North Klondike River Valley. Bud had started reading it, and now down on the broad gravel flats of the river where he could see out better, he could make out large boulders dotting the nearby low hills from the glacier's terminal moraine or leading edge.

Looking into the distance with no trees to obstruct his view, he could now see the Dempster snaking along to the horizon, and he once again felt that the vast panoramas of the North Klondike were similar to the landscape around Green River for their openness, though he knew there had never been any glaciers in that part of Utah.

Bud had read that after leaving Tombstone Territorial Park, the Dempster Highway ran through what's called Berengia, an ice-free area during the last ice age that extended across the Yukon and into Alaska and on to Siberia. It was in the rain shadow of the mountains and thereby got very little moisture, serving as a refuge for Pleistocene animals such as the mammoth and bison, which were able to cross the Bering Strait from Asia, which had become a grassy plain because of lower sea levels. The book had said that placer miners in the area often found ancient animal bones while digging for gold.

The river's main channel seemed to be running low, probably because it was autumn, Bud thought, and numerous shallow rivulets meandered back and forth along its wide gravel bed, typical of rivers in a glaciated landscape.

He picked up a stick and threw it for Lindie, who made a mad dash into the shallow water to retrieve it, then dropped it at Bud's feet. He was surprised, as he didn't think a dingo was very likely to play fetch, but someone had taught her how, probably William, he figured.

Bud now stood watching the Arctic light fade as the sun slowly set behind the distant hills, and he again felt the poignancy that seemed to have followed him from the distant landscape of home. And as he tried to picture wooly mammoths, giant sloths, dire wolves, and dire bears, he found himself more aware than usual of the nearby shadows and their mysteries.

Suddenly, Lindie crouched down as if to make herself invisible, just like in Bud's dream. Alarmed, his eyes followed where she was looking into the deep shadows along the riverbank, but he saw nothing. He quickly put her leash on, deciding it was time to go back to the cafe.

But just then, Lindie leaped into the air, and if it weren't for the leash jerking her back, Bud knew she would've been in serious trouble, for there, not more than 40 feet away, he could see the outline of one of the biggest bears he'd ever seen.

He froze, knowing to never run from a bear, yet wondering if Lindie might draw it to him, as he knew bears didn't like dogs and would often go after them.

Now the bear, seemingly unafraid, stepped from the shadows, where Bud could now see it was the largest black bear he'd ever seen. It seemed curious, its ears forward. It didn't gnash its teeth or make a popping sound, both of which Bud knew were signs of fear and possible aggression, but just stood quietly.

Bud told Lindie to sit, which she did, to his surprise. He then carefully and slowly took his camera from its pack. If he were going to die from a bear mauling in the Yukon, he would at least leave a few good photos of the bear for posterity.

It was a beautiful animal, and Bud managed to get a good half-dozen shots of it backlit by the pinks and reds of a Yukon sunset, the colors reflecting below it in the river, the tips of its hair glowing in the waning sun.

And as the bear stood looking at him, he felt a brief moment of connection with a creature of high intelligence, another being just trying to make a living on Planet Earth.

A feeling of exhilaration went though him, and as he put the camera down, he said softly, "Thank you for the photos. You're a beautiful animal, and I hope you don't eat me, but if you do, it was worth it just seeing you—well, maybe, anyway."

It now turned and disappeared into the bushes by the river, leaving him feeling the same kind of awe he'd felt on seeing Mount Monolith in dawn's light. He was thankful it hadn't chosen to come after Lindie.

Heading back to the Klondike Cafe, Bud could now see several vehicles parked in front, one he recognized as Shorty's Ford and the other as Stan's old pickup. Bud wasn't surprised to see Stan's truck, but he wondered why Shorty had come back.

But as Bud got closer, he slipped behind the bushes, for a Range Rover like Dougie's had just pulled up. He watched as two Mounties got out and entered the cafe, then soon came back outside with a handcuffed man between them, putting him in the back seat.

Bud was shocked, for it looked like they'd just arrested Shorty Doyle. He now recalled Dougie's words back in Green River:

"We want to find this man—we *will* find this man—and bring him to justice."

And just like when he'd thought the avalanche had caught Shorty, he again felt inept and incompetent, for he had no idea what to do next.

30

Still standing there in the bushes with Lindie, Bud recalled what Shorty had said earlier when he'd asked him how he could prove he was innocent, and in retrospect, Shorty's answer seemed simple: find the murderer.

He now wondered if the Mounties had finally found Anderson's body. Surely they had good reason to believe Shorty was guilty and wouldn't arrest him simply because he and Dougie didn't get along.

And why would they blame Shorty for William's murder? Had he somehow been in the vicinity, or had he and William been having some kind of disagreement?

Bud now walked back over to the cafe just as another vehicle pulled up. He was at first leery, wondering if it weren't more Mounties coming to arrest him, and he was relieved when Joe got out.

Lindie wagged her tail, and Joe stopped to pet her and say hello to Bud, then they all went inside. There, Lily and Stan were drinking tea, looking disconsolate. They seemed pleased to see everyone.

"They just came and arrested Shorty," Stan said. "Joe, since you're here, maybe you can go with me to his camp. No point in letting good supplies go to waste."

"Unbelievable," Lily said with disgust. "All you care about is getting Shorty's food. You could care less that he's been arrested."

"That's not true," Stan said defensively, his brows furrowed. "But no point in letting the bears get all that food when we could use it."

"They've been threatening to arrest him for some time now," Joe said.

"How do you know that?" Stan asked.

"It's no secret Shorty's been hiding out. You're the one supplying him, Pop. Didn't it occur to you he was hiding from someone?"

Stan shook his head. "He's up there doing field research, that's what he told me."

"Then why was he having you go to Whitehorse to get supplies instead of Dawson?" Lily asked, then answered her own question. "Because he was hiding out."

"I'm always the last one to know anything," Stan said dejectedly.

"Do you even know where his camp is, Pop?" Joe asked.

"No," Stan replied.

"Why did he come back to the cafe after getting his supplies?" Bud asked.

"Lily made him a big batch of popcorn balls, and he forgot them," Stan replied. "She lured him back."

"I hope they don't come back and arrest you for aiding and abetting a criminal," Lily said.

Bud got the distinct feeling they were enjoying gigging each other.

"Shorty didn't kill nobody," Joe now said. "Jimmy Mason told me he was out fishing and saw Mounties out by Pennington Station yesterday. I think they were out taking one last look around, and it appears they may have found something. All they have to do is ask me, and I can tell them who killed Willie, and probably that geologist, too."

Bud, who'd been silent, was now on high alert.

"You know who killed Willie?" Stan asked.

"That's why I came up here, Pops. I'm going to the Mounties. I could go to the Carcross detachment, but they won't take me seriously. Dougie McDougald in Dawson was Willie's sergeant. You might want to hold out on getting Shorty's supplies, cause he didn't do it, and they're going to have to let him go. Grady did it."

Lily gasped, and Stan looked shocked.

Now Bud spoke, "Joe, you must have some good evidence, or you wouldn't be going to the RCMP."

"I do, Bud. First, Grady was in Carcross the day Willie was killed. He never comes back down there 'cause he owes too many people money. That he was there in itself is highly suspicious. Then I found out later he "borrowed" his cousin's boat and took it out. He was gone for some time, long enough to get to Pennington Station and back."

Bud thought of the Baby Ruth candy-bar wrapper he'd found in the bushes there, then said, "I got the distinct feeling you were looking for someone besides Lindie when you found us out there. Was it Grady?"

Joe continued, "Yes. I had a hunch Grady may have killed Willie. He was known for being anti-government, and he hated the Mounties. He'd told his cousin he'd dynamited one of the microwave towers up the Dempster. When I found out he was in town, I got real suspicious."

Lily said, "Dynamited a microwave tower? What's wrong with that guy? Doesn't he realize that's our communications? Those poor people up in Eagle Plains and Inuvik, what about them?"

"He knew how to set a charge?" Bud asked.

"Yes, he worked at a gold mine when he was younger," Joe said. "But he's totally unstable. I hope he doesn't get a reduced sentence for some kind of mental thing."

Lily now said, "Unstable? Yes, I would say he is. Did I tell you he swore to kill the government guy who told us we had to upgrade our sewage system? I kind of felt sorry for the fellow, Luke Anderson was his name. He'd been out there studying the river for some time, and I know he felt we were harming the environment. He was just doing his job. He came by here with the news, and Grady about went ballistic on him. Stan had to get involved."

"He probably killed *him*, too," Joe said angrily. "Willie was with the

Dawson Detachment and he seldom came down our way, but the day before he was killed he called and told me he was taking someone out by boat on Bennett Lake, and he would stop by later. I can't recall who or why, and I'm not even sure he told me who it was. I got the feeling it had something to do with his job."

"Was he in uniform when he was killed?" Bud asked.

"Yes," Joe replied. "Well, I assume he was, though the Mounties wouldn't tell us anything. Willie was proud to be a Mountie and wore his uniform every chance he got."

"Did Grady know William?" Bud asked.

"Sure," Lily replied. "Like I mentioned, Grady worked for us for some time, and Willie would come by when he could. I can't believe Grady would kill him, especially since we'd made him a part of the family, well, as much as possible, given his temperament."

Joe said, "He was so anti-government after the roadhouse was shut down it wouldn't surprise me if he just aimed and shot when he saw the Mountie uniform, not knowing it was Willie."

"Shot?" Bud asked, surprised. "I thought William drowned."

"We were told he drowned," Lily said. "But who knows?"

"But if he drowned," Bud asked, "Why do they think it was murder?"

Joe replied, ""Nobody knows, Bud. I know there was more to it. Willie was an expert boatman and a strong swimmer. He grew up in Carcross. We spent our childhood out on Bennett Lake. He would've been the last person to drown out there."

Now Joe was silent, and Lily stood and put the teapot on the stove while Stan looked at the floor.

Joe finally said. "All I know is that Grady killed my brother, and it's time for the RCMP to get with it and arrest the right guy before he goes after someone else."

31

"Nothing personal, Bud, but I really wish you'd go back to the States," Sergeant Dougie told Bud over his desk in his office in Dawson. "If word gets out you're here illegally, I'll be held accountable for not arresting you. There's nothing you can do for Shorty at this point."

"I'm not even sure how to get back into the States, Dougie," Bud replied, Lindie at his feet. "If I go back through a border checkpoint, isn't the border guard going to ask why I'm not in the system as having entered Canada?"

"You might get lucky," Dougie replied. "But why are you in Dawson? You're just increasing the odds that one of my detachment will want to see your passport for some reason or another, and at that point, I can't give you immunity. And I didn't mean for you to wear that coat all over with people thinking you're a Mountie. Besides, Dawson isn't really your kind of town."

Bud had ridden into town with Joe, then gotten a room in a hotel, where he'd cleaned up and changed clothes. He'd talked Lily into letting him take Lindie, as he suspected he would be going home before too long and wanted to be with her. At the hotel, he'd been able to contact Wilma Jean, who had told him she was about ready to fly up and see what was going on.

Bud told Dougie, "I'm wearing the coat you gave me 'cause I gave my other coat away."

Dougie now looked pensive. "I'm going back to 'Berta soon."

Bud was surprised. "Are you getting transferred?"

"No, I'm retiring from the force. I've done well as a Mountie, making it to sergeant and all, but I want to be closer to my family, and my dad's offering me half the farm if I come down and help run it."

He then added, "Besides, this case is starting to get to me."

Bud whistled. "Well, I wouldn't have predicted you becoming a farmer. You do a good job as an LEO. What kind of crops?"

"Mostly wheat and canola. A little northwest of Calgary near a little town called Digsby."

"You'll enjoy farming after being up here. It's a whole different world from law enforcement. You need to get a couple of dogs, though, to really do it right."

"Dogs?"

"Yeah, so you have something to do when you're not working, play stick and all that. Dogs and farms go together."

Bud patted Lindie, again wishing he could take her home with him, then asked, "Was Joe able to convince you that Grady killed William?"

"No. Everything Joe presented was just circumstantial, though we *are* going to keep a close eye on Grady. But admitting to a crime that wasn't committed doesn't help the case."

"What crime?"

"Dynamiting a microwave tower. We have no evidence of such. Besides, we have good evidence that Shorty killed William, not Grady."

"Care to share what that evidence is?"

"No."

"Can I see Shorty?"

"No. He's in Whitehorse. There's no jail here in Dawson, except the old historic one. If you went to Whitehorse, they might let you see him, I really don't know. Actually, that's a good idea—go on down to Whitehorse, then back to Skagway. You can probably get back through the border at that point with no trouble. Remember, you won't be going through Canadian customs when you return, and who knows if the American border patrol will care where you've been. Surely your wife misses you."

Now Bud said, thoughtfully, "Dougie, I want to stay a little longer. I really think Shorty is innocent, and I have some ideas about what might be going on."

"Care to share them?" Dougie asked.

"Not quite yet," Bud replied. "But I think it has something to do with this."

He handed Dougie the rock sample he'd taken when they were up helping Jan.

"Remember this?" Bud asked.

"How could I forget?" Dougie replied, taking the sample, which had what appeared to be a diamond encrusted in the black rock. He added, "This is the stuff of dreams, if this is a real diamond."

"It is," Bud replied. "I stopped by the office of that big gold mining dredge out of town a ways. They had a guy there who said he was a mining geologist, and he said he thought it was kimberlite."

"You mean the stuff diamonds are found in, like in South Africa?"

"Exactly. Kimberlite comes from deep within the mantle and is the source of diamonds. It's the result of explosive volcanism—these kimberlite pipes just violently explode to the surface at over 500 miles per hour, and kimberlite can also be found in volcanic dikes, which is what we found. Nobody really understands it, but there are over 6,000 of these known pipes all around the world, though a lot of them don't bear diamonds. They form under high pressure and temperature within the mantle."

"Unbelievable," Dougie said, examining the rock.

Bud continued. "You can get what's called indicator placer deposits below these pipes and dikes with things like garnets, and I think Anderson found one that led him to the deposit where we found Jan. I haven't talked to her, but I suspect she found it while wandering around lost and then twisted her ankle. Is she still in the hospital?"

"No, she's back in Whitehorse. She's doing fine," Dougie replied. "But what good would this do anyone, since it's illegal to mine in the park?"

"Anderson and Shorty were doing government mapping up Wolf Creek. They were near the back side of Vantage Point, which is where we found Jan. Grizzly Creek is the drainage on the other side, just below Vantage Point. Anderson must've been up Grizzly Creek many times taking samples and studying the geology and came upon indicator materials or even loose diamonds that led him to the dike."

Dougie sat silent, then said, "I would never believe there were diamonds in the Tombstones if I hadn't seen it for myself."

Bud continued. "Shorty told me a little about the Tombstones when we were camped up there. They're made of syenite, which is an igneous material that punched upward into overlying sedimentary layers about 90 million years ago. As the material cooled, steep shrinkage cracks developed. I'm no geologist, but I think this is what led to the dike being accessible."

Now Dougie asked, "So you think Anderson found diamonds and was illegally mining them?"

"Possibly," Bud replied. "And I think it's all tied with his disappearance."

"Disappearance? Don't you mean death?"

"There's still no body, is there, Dougie?" Bud asked. "And just because you guys found a hand lens yesterday with Shorty's initials near where William was killed, well, that's evidence about as circumstantial as any Joe presented to you this morning."

Dougie was surprised. "Who told you about the lens?"

"Nobody, except Shorty said it had gone missing, and Joe said there were Mounties searching near Pennington Station. Shorty valued that hand lens highly, as it was a gift from someone he thinks a lot of. I think he may have been framed by whoever killed William. But Dougie, there's also this."

Bud now pulled the bear-claw necklace from his pocket and put it on the desk.

"Lily made each person in her family one of these. Her daughter's down in Horsefly, B.C., so I doubt if she's been around, but when I was in the cafe earlier, I noticed Lily and Stan were both wearing theirs, but Joe wasn't. This either belonged to Joe or William, unless you guys found William's on his body."

"Where did you find this?" Dougie asked.

"It was up on the slope near where the avalanche was triggered."

"Triggered?"

"Dougie, I've been working under the assumption we were in this together, that we both have the same outcome in mind, to find who murdered William and possibly Anderson. You and I both know that avalanche was set off. I understand not wanting to share evidence that could be used to cloak a killer, but this is different. Maybe it would be in the RCMP's best interest to be a little more forthcoming."

Bud now picked up the necklace and put it back in his pocket, saying, "I'm going to take Lindie for a walk, then maybe we can have lunch, if you know a good place. I still haven't had a chance to sample this poutine stuff you Canucks are so fond of. And we need to solve this case so I can take your advice and go home."

Dougie nodded his head in agreement, then watched grimly as Bud led Lindie out the door.

32

Bud sat in the office of the Dawson Mining Recorder at 1242 Front Street, Dawson City, Yukon Territory. He thought back to when he'd received the mining claim in the big envelope back in Green River. It seemed like years ago, so much had happened since.

A friendly looking guy sat across from Bud at a big desk that had a name placard that read "Mr. Pete Archibald." He was going through records on his computer while answering Bud's questions.

"Yes, the Mining Recorder Office does track Yukon gold claims, Mr. Shumway, and if you'll hang on just a minute, I'll bring yours right up."

Bud nodded appreciatively, now wondering if he'd done the right thing by leaving Lindie in the hotel room. He was hoping to have lunch with Dougie, and he knew the restaurants wouldn't allow dogs. He hoped this wouldn't take long.

Pete continued. "Yes, people still mine these hills for gold. We have record of about 80 small, family owned and operated mines still in operation in the Klondike, and over 13,500 placer claims. Oh, here's yours."

Bud replied, "Transferred from Jacob Doyle, right?"

"That's correct, and before that, Luke Anderson," Pete said.

"And before that?" Bud asked. "Wait, let me guess—William Walker?"

"You certainly know the history of your claim, Mr. Shumway."

"And before that, Luke Anderson again? And he was the original claimant, right?"

"Yes, that's correct."

Bud asked, "Is it unusual for a claim to have so many transfers?"

"Not at all," Pete replied. "Some people have 50 or more registered claims and do nothing but buy and sell. A lot of them are leased out to bigger companies. I know of one fellow who hasn't found one ounce of gold—he's not what we'd call a heavy hitter in the mining business—yet he makes a good living buying and selling claims."

"People still come up here thinking they'll get rich?" Bud asked.

"Oh yes," Pete shook his head. "Modern mining is as steeped in secrecy, mistrust, and betrayal as it was during the gold rush, when prospectors bribed officials to move a boundary or change the name on a claim. in fact, the Mounties were just in here not too long ago, wanting to see the record of this same claim you have here, though I have no idea why. But what can I do for you?"

"I want to transfer my claim to someone else," Bud replied, now wondering if the claim's history wasn't part of the evidence Dougie said they had for Shorty killing Anderson or even William. Maybe they thought Shorty was somehow after the claim. It would explain why they thought Bud was involved.

Pete now looked through a nearby filing cabinet and pulled out a sheet of paper that looked just like the one Bud had been carrying in his pack.

"Who do you want to transfer it to?"

"Lily and Stanley Walker," replied Bud. "But I just realized I don't have their address."

"Lily and Stanley out at the old Klondike Cafe? I can look it up. They're still out there, aren't they?"

"They are," Bud said.

"What I would give for a slice of Lily's Berry Delight pie," Pete said. "Someone should tell her to start delivering those to places around town. There are lots of people who would buy her baked goods."

"I'll mention it to her," Bud said.

Now Pete examined Bud's claim, saying, "You're from Green River, Utah?"

"I am," Bud replied. "Ever been there?"

"No, but a friend of mine grew up there."

"Would that be Shorty Doyle, AKA Jacob?" Bud asked.

"Yes, the one who sold you this claim. Where is he these days?"

Bud replied, "Last I heard, he was in Whitehorse."

"Oh. He told me last time I saw him he was moving back to the States, so I thought maybe he'd left already. I was hoping he'd come by and say goodbye first."

Bud paused. So, Shorty had been serious about going back to Green River. He hoped it wasn't too late.

Bud replied, "I'm sure he'll be back. He needs to get his stuff before he goes anywhere."

Pete now said, "OK, now I need to see your ID."

Bud pulled out his passport. Wally took a quick look then said, "It's now transferred. That'll be 30 loonies."

"Loonies? Do you take American dollars?"

"Yes, we do," Pete said. "Every place in Dawson takes American money because of all the tourists. We all use the Fair Exchange Rate, which is updated weekly. If it weren't for all the Yankee and European tourists, this would be a ghost town—it actually is, in the winter."

"It does seem kind of quiet," Bud replied.

"It'll be snowed in before long. The ferry will close soon, and that marks the end of the season."

"Ferry?"

"The George Black ferry across the Yukon. It's part of the road system, connects to the Sixty Mile or Top of the World Highway which goes to Alaska. If you haven't done the ferry yet, it's free—ride across and go visit the paddlewheel graveyard."

"What's that?" Bud asked.

Pete replied, "There was a time when paddlewheelers were the main type of transportation around here. Most of what's left at the graveyard are rotting away, but you can still see some of the actual paddlewheels, since they have metal skeletons. Just walk downstream a quarter mile or so from the campground by the river. But better go soon. The river's starting to ice up, and they'll be shutting everything down before long. You can't cross the Yukon after that until it freezes solid."

Pete was now finishing up, and he put the new transferred claim in a large envelope, just like the one Bud had received back in Green River, then handed Bud the old one, which had the word "Void" stamped on it.

"Do you want me to mail this to them, or do you want to hand carry it, assuming you're going out there?" Pete asked.

"Probably better to mail it," Bud replied. "And thanks for your help."

"Enjoy your stay in Dawson," Pete said. "And if you see Jacob, tell him to stop by."

Bud put the old claim back in his pack, then headed out the door, anxious to get back to Lindie, especially since Joe had told him she tore up things when left alone. He was now questioning why he'd left her, lunch or no, and decided to get back right away.

As he walked back to the hotel, he mulled over when Shorty told him that Anderson had sold the claim to a guy who thought he was being bilked and had demanded his money back. He now knew for sure that the guy was William, and he wondered if it didn't play into William's death somehow.

His intuition said it did, yet he had no idea why Anderson would kill him if he'd already refunded his money and sold the claim to Shorty. What would be his motive? Or had William attacked Anderson and he'd killed him in self-defense? But how could Anderson kill anyone when he was buried in an avalanche?

He knew he needed more information—it seemed like there was a piece missing, and he knew that piece was probably part of the evidence that Dougie said they had against Shorty. He needed to have lunch with Dougie and see if he could get him to tell him.

Bud now opened the door of his hotel room just in time to see Lindie trying to tug the curtains off their rods. The room was a mess —the bedclothes were on the floor, the garbage can was upended, and Lindie appeared to have even jumped up on the counter and tipped over the empty coffee pot.

Bud groaned. Even though it all looked like things he could fix, he knew that from now on, Lindie would be accompanying him wherever he went. Maybe it was for the best that he wasn't taking her back to Green River, though he suspected she would come around if given some security and the company of other dogs.

He and Dougie would just need to have a picnic or something outdoors, where he could take Lindie along.

He sighed as he started cleaning up the mess, Lindie watching, looking dejected and slowly wagging her tail.

33

Bud had tidied up the hotel room, then gone back to Dougie's office only to find him gone.

"We were told you might be coming by," said a small woman in a Mountie uniform. "I'm Inspector Kline. Sergeant McDougald asked me to give you this note. Nice coat, by the way," she smiled. "You're going to need it for this front coming through in a couple of days. It's going to be a doozie, according to the weather people. Early winter."

Dougie's note had apologized profusely for not being able to meet Bud for lunch, and had instead asked that he come back around six, when Dougie would pick him up. Sue, the photographer Bud had met on the plane, had invited them to her house for dinner, and Lindie was also welcome. Dougie had shared with her the story about sitting on the plane next to Bud, and she said she had something she wanted to show him.

Bud was somewhat disappointed. He wanted to meet one more time with Dougie and see if he would share what evidence they had against Shorty. It was beginning to feel like it was time to go home, and Bud knew he needed to get back.

He wasn't sure if the unsettled feeling he had was from some intuition or because of the front coming in, but things were starting to feel different. He couldn't quite put his finger on it, but it was almost like the feeling he'd get back home when winter was in the air and he wanted to make sure everything was buttoned up and ready.

The problem was, Bud had no idea where he would go next, though he was thinking of trying to get a ride back to Whitehorse. He knew he needed a plan for getting back to the States, and Whitehorse would not only put him six hours closer to home and near an airport, but where he could maybe somehow talk to Shorty. But somehow, going to Whitehorse didn't seem right.

It was only early afternoon, so he decided to walk around Dawson with Lindie, though he really just wanted to go back to the hotel and see if he could call Wilma Jean again, as well as Howie and maybe even Cassie. He'd only spoken to his wife for a moment when he got to the hotel, and he'd hardly even had time to catch up on how everyone was, especially her and the boys.

He led Lindie down the wooden boardwalk of the main part of town, the section where tourists could explore restored buildings from the gold rush, places like Diamond Tooth Gertie's Casino with its vaudeville shows, which billed itself as Canada's first legalized gambling hall.

Bud had wondered at Dougie's words saying that Dawson wasn't his kind of town, but the more he walked around, the more he was beginning to understand—Dawson was born in greed and even now existed mainly for gold mining and tourism. Bud had little interest in either.

He'd also read that Dawson had been the homeland of the Hän-speaking First Nations people, with their fishing and moose-hunting camp located there at the confluence of the Yukon and Klondike rivers. They'd basically been pushed out by the gold rush and moved downstream, where a large number of them were then wiped out by smallpox and typhoid brought in by the Stampeders. And the gold rush had a devastating impact on the environment, with massive soil erosion, water contamination, deforestation, and loss of native wildlife.

It wasn't a very palatable history, and Bud found it depressing, an unfortunate replay of much of European intrusion into the lives of indigenous peoples.

As Bud walked around, he occasionally met people who recognized Lindie and who would then ask about William. Most knew he was dead, though a few didn't, and it became awkward for Bud to explain why he had the dog. Finally, he decided to just go back to his room, realizing he wasn't enjoying himself.

As he walked into the hotel, he picked up a copy of the *Yukon News* from Whitehorse, with its headline: *Famous TV Personality Arrested for Murder*.

Bud took the paper to his room, where he sat down and read:

Geologist Jacob Doyle, host of the well-known CBC program, Deep Time, has been arrested and jailed in Whitehorse for suspected murder of Yukon Geological Survey employee Luke Anderson and RCMP Inspector William Walker. Crown prosecutor David McWhinnie stated that in spite of the case against Doyle, one should remember that he's innocent until proven guilty. The fact that Doyle has dual U.S.-Canada citizenship played into the decision to arrest him, as he was at risk for fleeing, said McWhinnie. The Crown will hear the case in the Yukon Territorial Court at an unspecified date.

Beneath the article were photos of both William and Anderson.

Bud had never seen a photo of William, and studying it, he could see he looked a lot like Lily, with kind eyes, high cheekbones, and dark hair. The photo was labeled "Courtesy of the RCMP," and Bud suspected it had been taken right after William had been hired, for he was wearing a Mountie uniform and had a look of pride on his face.

It brought it all home, Bud thought, from the theoretical to the concrete, seeing his photo, and he felt bad not only for Lily and Joe and Stanley, but for Lindie, as this had been the one person the little dingo had loved and trusted. Bud reached down and gently petted her head, and she took it as the OK to jump up on the bed next to him.

Now studying the photo of Luke Anderson, Bud noted that he certainly had the look of a geologist—fit and tan from being outdoors —but there was also something else there, something Bud couldn't quite put his finger on.

He finally took out his pocket knife and cut the article out, putting it in his pack, then pulled out his phone and dialed his friend Dr. Curt in Skagway. He would eventually call Wilma Jean, but he needed to make a couple of other calls first.

34

"Bud, I wish you were here to check out my peanut crop before it goes to market."

Bud had Howie on the phone.

"You actually got a crop?" Bud asked with amazement, as he'd been skeptical about being able to grow peanuts in Green River.

"I did. It's sitting right here in front of me on the table."

Bud laughed. It was great talking to Howie, and he realized how much he'd missed being back home, but right then, it seemed like a different planet.

Howie continued. "It's not much, but it does prove I was right—you can grow peanuts in Green River. And I'm going to make a batch of peanut brittle with them."

Bud replied, "I thought you said they were going to market."

Howie said, "They are. I harvested them, packaged them in a bowl, and am buying them from myself for a couple of bucks, and as the end consumer, I'm going to eat them."

Bud asked, "Don't you need to roast them first?"

"You're right. How do I do that?"

"I think you could just put them on some tin foil in the oven, maybe for about 20 minutes. Be sure to shell them first. But does this mean that next year you're planting all two acres in peanuts?" Bud asked.

Howie replied, "No, next year I'm going to try something different. Maybe pumpkins. But say, Sheriff, when are you coming home?"

"Is everything OK there, Howie? How's Maureen?"

"She's fine. There's nothing new going on, but we miss you. I go see the dogs every day, and I know they miss you, too. They don't seem to be quite as spunky."

"You mean bad," Bud laughed. "Howie, I've pretty much done about all I can here, so it won't be long."

"I hope you took lots of photos, Sheriff."

"I did, and I think I have some good ones."

As they said goodbye, Bud was suddenly overwhelmed with that same old poignancy—he felt it at different times for different reasons, but he knew all roads eventually led home. He'd always been this way, conflicted, some would call it, but when he was snug at home, he want to be out wandering, and when out wandering, he missed being home.

He now wondered again how he was going to get out of Canada, but maybe he could spend some time on the Internet here at the hotel and get some ideas. But first, it was almost time to go meet Dougie.

Bud washed up and put on a clean shirt, then fed Lindie, and grabbing her leash, headed for Dougie's office. The streets of Dawson were now dark, lit only by an occasional street light, and the dropping barometer from the incoming storm made everything seem somber, the air somehow feeling thicker, probably from the increasing humidity.

Dougie was at his office waiting, and they were soon on the other side of town at Sue's house, where she was busy preparing what smelled like a feast to Bud. He admired her comfy house, thinking of the bungalow back in Green River. He was beginning to feel like an exile, and the comforts so many took for granted weighed on him heavily.

"I'm used to having good home-cooked food, since my wife has a cafe," Bud said. "It's been awhile, and I can't tell you how good that smells. What is it, anyway?"

"Oh, it's an old tradition around my house," Sue replied. "Blood pudding."

Bud wasn't sure what blood pudding was, and it didn't sound very palatable, but he was polite enough to smile. He then repeated, "It sure smells good."

Sue laughed. "I'm just teasing. I know you Yanks aren't real big on stuff like that. Actually, we're having a nice roast with baked potatoes and salad, but Dougie asked if I would also make some poutine, since you've never had any. You can't come to Canada and not have poutine."

"Sounds fantastic," Bud replied. "Are these photos yours?" He nodded towards a wall of beautiful framed photos of the aurora.

"Yes, the Aurora Borealis is my specialty. According to the aurora forecast center up at the University of Fairbanks, we're going to have a good display tonight. When Dougie told me about you and pointed out we actually kind of knew each other from the plane ride, I thought it would be a nice thing to have you up for dinner. Afterwards, we can go up on Midnight Dome and take photos. If I recall correctly, you told me that's why you were coming up here."

"I've always wanted to get some good photos of the aurora," Bud answered. "Maybe you can give me some tips."

"I would be happy to," Sue replied. "Oh, here's Jules, my husband, back from Whitehorse. He teaches at Yukon College three days a week. I'm retiring soon, then we're moving up there."

"Sounds like Whitehorse is the place to be," Bud said. "Though I guess Dougie's going to Alberta, not Whitehorse."

"Both are lots warmer than Dawson," Dougie said. "Nice seeing you, Jules," he added.

Sue introduced Bud to Jules, who then said, "Let's eat," as he helped Sue bring dinner to the table.

And as Bud sat there with them, eating the most delicious dinner he'd had in ages, slipping bites of roast under the table to Lindie, he again realized how much he missed his home and family in Green

River. He'd been basically living like a homeless person since he'd left, except for his stay in the hotel, and it was beginning to wear on him. He didn't know how people who were truly homeless, like Grady, could keep it together both physically and mentally, and he knew some didn't. It was a harsh way to live, he thought.

After trying the poutine, which Bud then got the recipe for, they finished everything off with tea and Nanaimo bars, which Bud also got the recipe for.

"Everyone ready to go?" Sue now asked, and they were soon winding up a long steep road to Midnight Dome above town, the aurora twisting above them like a giant green snake.

35

Finally on top, they got out, and stretched below them were the lights of the town of Dawson, its fewer than 2,000 souls all that held the wilderness back. Bud could make out the mighty Yukon River glowing in the light of the aurora, the Klondike River merging with it just below and to their left.

A picnic table and old bench were at the top of the dome, and Bud could see the lights of communication towers farther up the slopes at the top.

"Be sure your camera is really stable before you start," Sue now said, taking out her camera and tripod. It's also important to try to focus on a bright star like Polaris, because then the aurora will be in focus also, as much as it can be, moving around like it does."

Bud began taking photos as Sue gave him more tips, checking out what he'd taken and offering advice. But before long, the lights began to fade away.

"Clouds are coming in," Dougie remarked. "The leading edge of the storm they promised us. Looks like we're done for the night."

Bud put his camera away, saying, "I think I got some great shots anyway. It's an amazing sight. Thanks for a great evening, Sue. But Dougie, as you advised, I'm going to be leaving Dawson soon."

Dougie replied with surprise, "Leaving? I thought you were going to prove Shorty's innocence before you left."

"I can't get any further without knowing what you guys are basing his arrest on. As an LEO, I'm used to being in the inside circle of investigation. It's pretty much impossible to solve anything without knowing what all the evidence is."

Sue now said with concern, "Dougie won't tell you what they found? Why not, Dougie?"

Dougie sounded irritated. "He may be in law enforcement in the States, but up here, he's just a commoner, and the rules are the rules. You know that, Sue."

"I do know that. But we're dealing with someone who's a professional and may have evidence we don't know about. What if Bud has something that can prove Shorty's innocent? Would you hang the guy because Bud's not a Mountie?"

Bud now said quietly, "I think I do have something that can prove Shorty's innocent. But I need to know what evidence you have against him, as it could change my mind."

The wind was now starting to pick up, and Dougie said, "We need to call it a night. This storm's moving in."

Sue now sounded angry. "Dougie, we've seen this in you before, and I know it's why the Commissioner has been pressuring you to retire. You're letting your own emotions and biases get in the way."

"Alright," Dougie said. "You're right, I'm being stubborn just because Shorty and I don't get along. I'll tell you what we found, Bud, but then I want to know what your so-called evidence is."

"It's a deal," Bud replied, holding Lindie close to him, as she was now getting restless.

"First, you asked about a bear-claw necklace, if William was wearing one. The answer is no, we didn't find one, but that's neither here nor there. Second, the coroner found abrasion marks on William's ankles and wrists, as if he'd been tied and had struggled. He definitely drowned, but he was also tied at some time, and Shorty had been seen not far from where we found William's body."

Bud was astonished. "How could Shorty be down there when he was up in the Tombstones? Who saw him?"

Dougie replied, "I have a statement from Grady Johnson saying he saw him at the same time William was down there. It's pretty convincing. After Joe told me his concerns, we found Grady and talked to him. And you keep asking about Anderson's body. Well, I also have a damning piece of evidence—when Shorty gave me Luke's hat that he'd found at the avalanche site, he didn't realize that it had a note from himself stuck in the headband."

"A note?" Bud asked. "In Shorty's handwriting?"

"Yes. Definitely his handwriting, we even had it analyzed."

"What did it say?"

"It basically said that if Luke kept doing what he was doing, he was going to end up in Hell and no one would be able to find his remains. It's a dire threat, and I know Shorty set off that charge."

"What was Anderson doing that Shorty didn't like?" Bud asked, though he was pretty sure he already knew.

"Arguing over who had found the oldest rock. It was hurting Shorty's reputation."

Bud was quiet, then took something from his pack and handed it to Dougie, saying, "OK, here's my evidence, and I think you'll find it's pretty convincing."

He handed Dougie the plastic bag with the bloody piece of jeans he'd found near Pennington Station.

Bud said, "Dougie, send this to your lab, have them analyze the blood."

"Where did you get this?" Dougie asked.

"Pennington Station. There's a pair of jeans rolled up in the corner inside the building. Get your guys down there ASAP before this storm gets bad to retrieve them. This patch came out of them."

"Whose are they, William's?"

"No, I don't think so. I think they belong to William's killer."

"Shorty?"

"No." Bud paused, then said, "Look, it's late. We can talk more tomorrow. I'm going to stop by your office in the morning. I'd like to see that note from Shorty."

Bud could tell Dougie wasn't happy. They took Sue home, then Dougie dropped Bud and Lindie off in front of the hotel, not saying a word the entire time.

Bud now felt unsettled, and he knew it was partly from the incoming storm, but he also felt like he'd been playing a game of one-upmanship with Dougie, and he didn't like the way it made him feel.

And thinking about what happened next, he decided he hadn't been himself and wasn't as aware of his surroundings as he normally was, but was tired and distracted.

For as he opened the door to the hotel lobby, Lindie suddenly leaped backward, pulling the leash from his hand and taking off into the night, leaving Bud standing in the wind, aghast.

36

After several hours wandering the dark and desolate streets of Dawson City looking for Lindie in the cold wind, Bud finally had to admit defeat.

It seemed like just another in a series of gloomy incidents that were taking their toll on him, and he finally went back to the hotel and crawled into bed, exhausted.

He had no idea why Lindie would run off like that, and it made him doubt his ability to take care of the little yellow dingo. He'd thought they were bonding pretty well, and she'd seemed to really take to him, but if she was that unpredictable, he knew he wasn't enough of a dog trainer to know what to do. Maybe it was her wild heritage, Bud thought, knowing Carolina Dogs didn't have millennia of domesticity behind them like other dogs.

He didn't sleep well, dreaming of Lindie in various kinds of trouble, from bears to traps to even falling in the mighty Yukon River in the dark. He awakened several times and got up, walking around outside the hotel, thinking maybe she'd come back, but never seeing hide nor hair of her.

It was morning when he heard someone tapping on his door. He quickly got up and got dressed, thinking it was probably the maid wanting to clean, as he was supposed to be checking out soon.

To his surprise, there stood Grady, Lindie at his side, wagging her tail and seeming happy to see Bud.

Bud was soon hugging her, asking, "Where did you find her?"

"I was driving by Willie's old house this morning and she was sitting on the step."

"Poor Lindie," Bud said, stroking her head. "But how did you know to bring her back here?"

Grady shifted back and forth on his feet. "I saw you come in here a time or two."

Bud replied, "Grady, thanks for bringing her back. But I thought you were pretty much living in Whitehorse these days. Are you back in Dawson for good?"

"I don't live anywhere," Grady replied. "I keep hoping Stan and Lily will let me come back to the Klondike Cafe. I mean, I could stay in the back or something, but I'm afraid I've burned my bridges with them."

"Well, come on in. Let me get my stuff together since I'm checking out, then I'll buy you breakfast if you know a place where we can take Lindie inside."

"We can put her in my truck," Grady offered. "She can't get out."

"She might tear it up," Bud replied.

"Nah, I've taken Willie places in it and she was fine when we left her for awhile. She'll know where she is."

Bud and Grady were soon at Dino's Restaurant, and Bud couldn't help but notice how hungry Grady seemed.

"Order whatever you want," Bud said. "Call it repayment for the harmonica lesson."

Grady laughed and ordered two Alaska Burgers, which was a fish sandwich with fries, while Bud sat drinking a coffee called Tundra Mud. He liked the blend so much he bought a pound to take home.

"Say, Grady, would you mind taking me out to the Klondike Cafe? Pull over at the station and let me fill your tank for you on the way."

Grady, who had been enjoying talking about music with Bud, now seemed suspicious. "If you don't mind me asking, why are you going out there?"

"I have to take Lindie back. I'm leaving today."

"I thought she was your dog now," Grady said.

"I want to keep her, but Lily and Stan want her. I think there's a connection with her and William in their minds."

Grady shook his head. "She belongs with you. Just look at her. She really likes you. Willie would want you to have her."

"But she did run away last night, Grady. Maybe she'd be happier around people she's used to, like Stan and Lily and Joe. She spent a lot of time with them when William would visit."

"Oh, I don't know," Grady said. "They never paid her much mind. She was Willie's dog. You know, you remind me of Willie. He and I were good friends. He was a real kindhearted guy, in spite of being a Mountie."

"I understand why you feel like you do, Grady, but not all government types are bad," Bud said.

"I liked them just fine until that geologist guy shut the cafe down," Grady said.

"Say, Grady, rumor has it you saw that geologist guy down by Bennett Lake. Is that true?"

Grady's brows furrowed. "Who told you that?"

"Sergeant McDougald."

Grady now pulled the truck over, and Bud was sure he was going to ask him to get out.

"You sure seem thick with the Mounties for not being one," Grady said. "I just talked to McDougald, and now you know all about it."

Bud replied, "I had dinner with him and the RCMP photographer last night. We were going to take aurora photos, but the weather clouded up. Grady, an innocent man is in jail right now in White-horse based on what you told Dougie. I don't know what you said, but how could you have seen Shorty Doyle down at Pennington Station when he was up in the Tombstones?"

"I never told McDougald I saw Doyle. I didn't see Doyle."

"And you know what Doyle looks like?"

"I've seen him on TV, like everyone else."

"And you've been to his camp," Bud added, remembering the candy-bar wrapper he'd found there.

Grady replied, "I was desperate. I borrowed a little food a couple of times, figuring he'd blame it on the bears. I don't like living like that, I can tell you."

"Who did you tell McDougald you saw?"

"I don't know, 'cause I don't know the guy's name," Grady replied. "They just asked me if I saw the geologist, and I said yes."

"They never told you his name or showed you a photo or even asked you for a description?"

"Nope."

"And the geologist you saw was the same fellow who shut down the cafe, right? Luke Anderson?"

"That's right. So you're saying they put Doyle in jail based on what I told them?"

"It appears so," Bud shook his head. "But what was Anderson doing when you saw him at Bennett Lake?"

"I borrowed my cousin's boat to go fishing. I was tired of being broke and hungry, so I figured I'd catch a few to eat and a few to sell. I was out on the water, when I saw two guys out in a boat, not too far from shore. I figured they were out fishing, too. They drifted their way and I drifted mine, but then I saw they had a dog with them. Now, I know Willie sometimes would take Lindie out fishin' when he came to Carcross, so I wondered if it wasn't him taking someone out."

"Did you catch up with them?" Bud asked.

"I did and I didn't," Grady replied. "They had beached the boat by the time I got over there, and I could hear someone yelling, and a dog barking its head off. I beached my boat and got out, heading for the sound, when everything got quiet, though the dog was still barking. I decided I would be smart not to barge in on something that wasn't my business, so I walked up the tracks a ways, listening."

"Was this by Pennington Station?" Bud asked.

"Yes, right by it. I finally caught a glimpse of someone, so I hid in the bushes. That geology guy walked right by me, the same guy who shut down the cafe. I really wanted to punch him out, but I restrained myself. I finally went back to my boat and the other boat was gone, though I thought I saw the dog running farther down the beach as if looking for someone."

"Could that dog have been Lindie?"

"Yeah, it could've been her. Right size and color and all. After I heard she was missing, I wished I'd gone back and looked."

"Do you think the guy in the boat with the geologist was William?"

"At the time, I didn't think much about it, except thinking it was odd. But after I heard Willie was killed, I was pretty sure it had been him."

"Why didn't you go to the Mounties?" Bud asked.

"Well, by then I was trying to survive in Whitehorse and had had my fill of the RCMP, to be honest."

"Grady, is there any way you would go back to McDougald and tell him all this?"

"I don't know. I'm getting more and more to where I want less and less to do with those guys."

Grady now pulled back onto the road, then stopped at the gas station.

Bud continued. "Grady, McDougald is bound and determined to hang Shorty for something he didn't do. What you saw could change that. You have the power to keep the RCMP from ruining a man's life. Is there anything I could do to help you decide to go talk to McDougald again?"

"I don't know, Bud. I just don't know."

Bud got out and filled Grady's tank using his card, then they drove on, saying nothing until they finally pulled into the drive of the Klondike Cafe.

Bud got out, Lindie still on the leash, then hoisted his pack over his shoulder. "You might as well come inside," he said, opening the cafe door and nodding to Grady, who followed him in.

And as they entered the dim light of the old cafe where Lily sat reading and Stan worked a crossword puzzle, it occurred to Bud that Grady may have described the play in great detail to Dougie, but that Dougie got the main character wrong—unfortunately for Shorty Doyle—and it appeared it wasn't just a dress rehearsal.

37

"Well, if it isn't Mr. Utah!" exclaimed Lily as Bud and Grady walked in the door. "And Grady," she added without enthusiasm.

"We wondered if you were coming back," Stan said.

Lily replied, "We did not! We knew you'd bring Lindie back. Are you getting ready to leave now that Shorty's in jail?"

Bud replied, "I'm going to talk to Sergeant McDougald one more time, Lily, and after that, there's not much more I can do." He then added, "But Lily, I have something you and Stan may want."

He pulled the bear-claw necklace from his pack and handed it to Lily.

"I believe this belonged to William. It seems to me something you'd want to keep."

Lily's voice had a catch as she asked, "Where did you get this?"

Bud replied, "Up above the avalanche that supposedly killed Luke Anderson."

Now Stan asked, "Are you saying that Willie had something to do with the geologist's death?"

Bud asked, "Did William know how to set off explosives?"

Stan replied, "Every red-blooded man in the Yukon knows how to set off explosives. Finding that necklace up there doesn't prove a thing. Willie would never do something like that."

Bud replied, "Well, Stan, I agree. I don't think William would do something like that, from what I've learned about him. I think it was planted by the man who killed William as a way to try to implicate him."

"A red herring," Lily said.

"What's a red herring?" Stan asked.

Lily now replied with disdain, "Stanley, you should try reading a book now and then. A red herring is something used to divert people from seeing what's really going on, a dead-end kind of thing."

Bud nodded his head, saying, "In this case, though, it's more of a direct plant to try to make William look guilty. The problem is, it didn't work because a marmot got involved."

"A marmot?" Stan asked.

Bud replied, "Yes, it took the necklace partway down its hole and the Mounties never found it."

"Do the Mounties think Willie killed the geologist?" Lily asked with concern.

"I don't think so," Bud replied, glancing at Grady. "They're still thinking Shorty did it."

"That's too bad," Stan said.

Bud thought back on transferring the claim, and he knew it was too soon for them to have received it, and he'd prefer to be gone by then anyway. He knew, based on what Shorty had told him, that the claim had a good chance of being productive, and he simply hoped they could find some good in it.

Bud now said, "Lily, I want to relay some information to you from Pete, the guy at the claims office. He says for you to start making baked goods and selling them in town. He says he really misses your Berry Delight pie."

Lily looked pleased, then said, "Now that we have Willie's insurance money from the RCMP, I can maybe invest in the stuff I need to set up a bakery. I think I could do pretty well."

"I know you could," Grady said, speaking for the first time. He waited a moment, then said, "You know, I quit drinking. Maybe I could be of some kind of help around here to you guys, try to make it up a little, you were so good to me."

Lily and Stan both looked skeptical, yet open to the idea.

"You boys want some popcorn balls?" Lily said, handing Grady a platter. Grady took one, but Bud declined, saying, "I'm going to be heading out now."

He handed Lindie's leash to Lily, saying, "I'll sure miss her."

Bud didn't know what else to say, so he turned to the door, hoisting his pack over his shoulder. The little dog pulled, trying to follow him, but Lily held her tight.

"We'll treat her well, don't you worry," Lily said. "And thanks again for finding her."

Bud nodded his head, not wanting them to see the tears in his eyes, and walked out the door.

To his surprise, Grady was behind him, saying, "I'll give you a ride into Dawson. I need to go talk to Sergeant McDougald."

Bud wiped his eyes on his sleeve and got into Grady's truck, trying not to dwell on the little dingo face watching him from the window of the Klondike Cafe.

38

"Dougie, I hate to tell you this, but you've totally misinterpreted Shorty's note to Anderson. It's actually kind of funny."

Bud sat in Dougie's office reading the note, Grady in the chair next to him. Sue was also there, sitting in a chair next to the window.

Bud was amazed at how clueless Dougie seemed to be, totally lacking in the understated humor Shorty was so good at. He read the note again:

Luke,

Keep it up and you're going to end up in the Hadean where no one will be able to find your gneiss remains.

Jacob

PS Don't forget that it's the in thing among field geologists working in the Canadian shield to wear fishing vests.

"I don't get why you think this is funny," Dougie said in his defense. "Threatening someone isn't humorous."

"It's tongue in cheek, Dougie. First of all, these guys are looking at the oldest rocks on the planet. The oldest geologic age is the Hadean, when Earth was a hot melting ball of fire, and the name of that era comes from the word Hades. And gneiss is the type of rock they're finding—the technical term is *gneiss remains*. And seriously, Dougie, the line about geologists wearing fishing vests is about as non-threatening as it gets—it's pure Shorty. That kind of humor is partly why Shorty's TV show was so popular."

Sue's lips were taut, and Bud could see she was displeased. "This is what you based Shorty's arrest on?"

Dougie looked tired and defeated. "I've been told I don't always interpret things like others do," he said. "I just don't see the humor in some things. But it all seemed to add up—Grady's testimony, the fact that Anderson and Doyle were feuding, the claim, Shorty's hand lens, the blast marks at the avalanche..." His voice trailed off.

"The same way you jumped to the conclusion that I knew where Shorty was simply because he transferred a claim to me, when the truth was, I hadn't had contact with him for three decades or more," Bud reminded Dougie.

Dougie replied, "I've done well here with the Mounties. So one makes a few mistakes..."

Sue said, "Shorty didn't make *any* mistakes, and you're ready to hang him." She then held up a recorder. "Anyone object to my recording all this?"

Now Dougie seemed to recover his equilibrium. "I still think he's guilty. You tell me who else had a motive to kill Anderson? And I think William got involved and knew what was going on, that's why his necklace was up there at the avalanche site. And the history of that mining claim tells a story. Shorty killed Anderson, then killed William because he knew too much."

Bud replied, "Anderson stole that necklace and planted it there to implicate William and confuse you, and it looks like he succeeded. He did the same thing with Shorty's hand lens—stole it, then left it near where he killed William. How do you account for what Grady just told you about seeing Anderson down at Bennett Lake, not Shorty? It sounds to me like Anderson's not even dead."

"Can he prove he saw Anderson? Or that he was even down there when he said he was? How do I know he's not covering for Shorty?"

"Because I found a candy-bar wrapper there, exactly where Grady said he was, and it's the kind Grady eats, a Baby Ruth."

"Talk about circumstantial evidence," Dougie replied.

"Maybe you consider this to be circumstantial also?"

Bud now handed Dougie a copy of the photo he'd taken of the hikers getting on the train.

He added, "Look carefully. There's a date stamp on the photo, and the train is clearly visible. You can ask the Yukon Railway exactly when they picked up these Chilkoot hikers, and they'll confirm it."

Dougie studied it for awhile, then said, "I don't understand why this is important."

Bud said patiently, "See the last hiker getting on the train? See how heavy his bag looks? He doesn't look like your typical hiker, does he? Here's a zoomed-in copy. That's Luke Anderson, and his bag is heavy because it's full of diamonds—Tombstone Territorial Park diamonds. I found one of those diamonds on the tracks. And he'd just killed William Walker a few days before. He intended to kill him all along, as he was the only one who knew Anderson was leaving the country and was still alive, not dead in the avalanche. Anderson tied William and then threw him in the lake, flipped his boat, and after he'd drowned, he took off the ropes so it would look natural, except he forgot to put his life vest back on him. That may have been intentional, to make it look like he wasn't wearing it, as it's hard to drown with one on. That patch of jeans I gave you has Anderson's blood on it. Did you send it to the lab yet?"

Dougie was silent.

Sue now asked, "Did you send anyone out to recover the jeans in Pennington Station? Could we get on that right away before this big storm shuts everyone down?"

"I'll call the Carcross Detachment right away," Dougie said.

"I'll do it," Sue said, obviously irritated. "And I may call the Commissioner while I'm at it."

Dougie, looking defeated, now asked, "Why would the jeans have Anderson's blood? Shouldn't it be William's?"

Bud replied, "Because Anderson forgot about the dingo. Lindie tore into him and bit his legs while he was tying William. After it was all done, he knew he couldn't board the train covered with blood and with his jeans all torn, so he changed and left them at Pennington Station. He wanted to get out of the country ASAP after leaving Dawson so nobody would see him, and that meant he had to spend several days out after killing William, as the train wouldn't pick up the hikers for awhile, so he had a pack with extra clothes and supplies. It takes three to five days to hike the Chilkoot, so he had to time it just right. You may not be able to match the DNA on the jeans with Anderson's yet, but you will, if you'll retrieve them and get them to the lab, and you'll find that patch I gave you was torn from them."

"How will we be able to match it with no DNA sample from Anderson?"

"Because we can get a DNA sample."

Dougie asked in surprise. "How?"

"He's in the Anchorage Hospital being treated for sepsis from dog bites."

Dougie looked shocked. "He's not dead?"

"No, but he may be soon. Sepsis is very serious."

"How do you know all this?"

Bud replied, "I have a friend who's a doctor in Skagway. I called him on a hunch. He treated Anderson after he got off the train, then sent him to the bigger hospital up north, as he was in serious condition—it had been several days since Lindie had bit him and his legs were infected. Because I'm an LEO in the States, the hospital is required to release information when I request it. The police in Anchorage are waiting for a call from you to detain him so he can't leave the hospital, though he's currently in no condition to do so."

"Another important call to make," Sue said. "But how about the avalanche?"

Bud replied, "Anderson had set up the explosives before he and Shorty were even up there. He tossed his hat into the trees where he hoped Shorty would find it, then climbed back up the slope, waited for Shorty to be out of harm's way, then set off the charge. He put William's necklace in a place where he figured the Mounties would find it, tying the explosion to William. He'd made sure everyone knew about how unhappy William was with the claim business, so supposedly William had a motive to murder Anderson. The problem was, the Mounties didn't find the necklace, because a marmot had dragged it halfway down its hole. I'm sure Anderson figured if the William thing didn't work, Shorty would make a good backup suspect, which he did, since a lot of people believed they hated each other."

Bud continued. "Anderson had now pulled off his own supposed murder and could proceed with his plan. By making everyone think he was dead, he also knew he wouldn't be a suspect in William's murder."

"But why would Anderson do all this?" Grady asked.

Bud replied, "Anderson wasn't all that interested in gold, because he knew how much work panning was, and a hard-rock mine entailed even more and called for investment capital. Anderson was pretty much happy with his lot in life as a government geologist with the Yukon Survey. But while out with Shorty, doing their work, Anderson stumbled upon the dream of every treasure seeker— diamonds. He didn't breathe a word of it to anyone, just quietly came back up and dug when he could, always careful to hide the evidence and make it look like he was doing work for the Survey. He couldn't file a claim, as he was in the Territorial Park, and he didn't want anyone coming around. He knew he was either going to have to take the gems out of the country to sell or somehow find someone else who would. And as a geologist, he knew they were high quality."

Bud continued. "We know William was motivated to help his parents, and a gold claim might do the trick, so when he somehow found out Anderson had one for sale he bought it, but then returned it. This was probably how he and Anderson hooked up in the first place, and when Anderson realized he needed help, he went to William. Given how proud William was to be a Mountie, I doubt very much if he knew about the diamonds and probably helped Anderson unknowingly."

Bud paused to catch his breath, then continued. "So, Anderson had collected enough diamonds that he was ready to leave Canada. The quickest way out was to fly, but he didn't think that he could get the diamonds out in his luggage, and he was probably right, plus there would then be a record of him as being alive and crossing the border. So, ironically, he studied the maps and decided the best way out was the way I came in, via Skagway. But in order to avoid the border patrol at Fraser, he had to go down the lake and then catch a ride on the train, the exact opposite of what I did. He probably called the train and found they were picking up the hikers at the end of the Chilkoot at Bennett Lake."

"So, Anderson had a plan. He would make it look like he himself had been killed, and William would be the suspect. Then he'd make it look like William had accidentally drowned, and now there would be no more suspect and the case would be closed. William couldn't tell anyone where Anderson had gone. But the one thing he hadn't planned on was Lindie."

"After getting bit, Anderson changed clothes, made it to the train, and got on board. I'm sure he planned to get a float plane into Alaska. It's easy to avoid customs if you make it to Skagway. But Lindie had put a pretty good dent in both legs, and they started getting infected. Dog bites are one of the worst things you can get for infection if you don't clean them up right away, as dogs have a lot of bad bacteria in their mouths. And because he was running scared and trying to lie low, Anderson neglected to go to a clinic and get disinfected and stitched up. The Detachment at Carcross went in to investigate William's death when they got a report of a body in the lake. William's body wasn't found that close to Pennington Station, as it had drifted some, so they never saw Lindie, nor Anderson's jeans."

"I'm leaving Canada now," Bud finished, standing. "I've done all I can. I hope you'll see fit to release Shorty, given what Grady and I have told you and the photo of Anderson, and I know the DNA will match."

Sue now held up the recorder. "I'm sure the Commissioner will want to release him after I present all this," she said.

As Bud pulled his pack over his shoulders, Sue studied the photo of Anderson on the train, then said, "I know you got some photos you didn't plan on, but I hope you also got some you wanted. Safe travels."

Bud shook hands with everyone, then walked out the door.

39

Bud stood on the banks of the mighty Yukon River, waiting for the ferry to come across. He couldn't recall ever seeing a river as wide, and it seemed to almost be alive, its waters reaching and splashing at his feet with small chunks of ice driving against the banks as if wanting to come ashore. He knew its waters would soon be still, in the frozen grip of another Yukon winter.

He could see the ferry about one-third of the way across, riding so low on the water that it looked as if it might be sinking. It held only a single car, as well as the ferry attendants, and Bud knew it was nearing its final run of the season, as the ice was beginning to hinder its passage. It wouldn't be long before the only way to cross the river would be by walking across its frozen surface.

The ferry arrived, and the car drove off onto the muddy river bank, then the attendant signaled for Bud to get on. He thought for a moment he was going to step into the water, as the ferry surged a bit as he was getting on, but he was soon safely aboard. The ferry waited for a moment to see if anyone else would come, then began fighting its way back across the river.

Bud felt apprehensive. He wasn't much of a swimmer, and it seemed like the river was as likely to swallow them up as to let them cross. Once on the other bank, he sighed as he stepped off the boat.

He was now wondering if he was doing the right thing by leaving this way, and the attendant's words didn't make him feel any better.

"This is our last crossing for the season," the man said. "Are you sure you want to stay over? You won't be able to come back across for a month or more until the river freezes up."

"I'm sure," Bud said without much conviction.

"Are you staying at the Yukon River Campground or something?" The man asked with concern, referring to one of the few businesses on this side of the Yukon, though it looked closed to Bud.

"No, I'm going on up the road," Bud replied. "To Chicken, Alaska."

The man now sounded even more concerned. "You're taking the Sixty Mile? Is someone meeting you up the road?"

Bud figured that the man was referring to the distance to the border. He knew it would be a long walk if he couldn't get a ride.

"I've been told there are a lot of moose hunters along the highway this time of year coming in from Alaska. I'm hoping to catch a ride."

"Well, that's a pretty iffy proposition," the fellow said. "Are you sure you want to do this? Hop on board and go back to Dawson. You can catch a bus and go to Alaska through Beaver Creek. There's a big storm coming in."

"I think I'll be alright," Bud replied. He knew if he didn't get going soon, his reservations would turn into fears, and he felt he just needed to get on with things.

"Are you sure customs is still open?" The man persisted. "If the border station is closed, you won't be seeing anybody for a long long time, until next spring. I don't think I've ever seen anyone trying to walk the T.O.W. this late in the season, if ever. It seems kind of suicidal, to be honest."

"The T.O.W.?" Bud asked.

"What Alaska calls the Top of the World Highway, but what we Yukoners call the Sixty Mile. And that's exactly what it is. It's just mile after mile mostly above timberline, no protection from the elements, and it's gonna be really windy this time of year—and cold. It's nothing but big high rolling hills flanked with clusters of scraggly trees, where's there's trees at all, all the way to Poker Creek."

"That's the customs station, right?" Bud asked.

"Yes. The Canada side is called Little Gold Creek, but they're in the same building. I'm telling you, you're crazy to take off walking out here this time of year, especially with a storm coming in off the Gulf of Alaska. Those are the worst."

Bud just shrugged his shoulders. "I'll be OK," he said, then thanked the guy for his concern and headed up the highway, leaving the ferry operator shaking his head.

He'd intended to go see the sternwheeler graveyard but had lost interest. All he wanted to do now was get going, his pack heavy with all the supplies he'd bought in Dawson after leaving Dougie's office.

He'd told no one his plan, and at this point in time, Bud didn't really care. He knew the Poker Creek station was probably his only hope of getting back into the States without a hassle, and he was hoping it would be closed so he could just walk around it. It was the second-highest border crossing in the U.S., and it closed when the first snows flew.

Interestingly enough, Bud had read that although the two border stations shared the facility, they were actually in different time zones. It looked pretty rustic in the photos he'd seen on the Internet, a large green building.

Bud was well-equipped food-wise, and he'd bought more cold-weather gear in Dawson. He knew that if he walked a little more than 10 miles a day, he could get to Poker Creek in less than a week, and he knew it would be impossible to get lost, as all he had to do was walk down the gravel highway. After that, a few more miles to Chicken and he'd be home free, as the town was populated year-round by a few hardy souls. From there, it would be a straight shot into Anchorage. He'd bought enough freeze-dried food and fuel for his little stove to last two weeks, and he hoped he could find water occasionally.

Looking back on it all later, Bud could see the folly of such an enterprise, but at the time, he felt strong and capable, and he truly was worried about crossing the border.

But something much larger factored into it all, and he realized later that he was depressed over losing Lindie. He'd become really attached to the little dingo, and having heard that Lily and Stan didn't pay her much mind hadn't helped things. He'd actually entertained the thought of dognapping her at one point, then decided it wasn't a good way to handle things.

He also wondered later if he hadn't made her into a symbol of everything he missed back home—his wife, Hoppie, Pierre, and the security of the bungalow and his own culture.

Be that as it may, he felt he had no choice but to accept things as they were, but he also knew he needed to walk it off, and this route would certainly allow him to do that.

He hoisted his pack and started up the road, which immediately began to climb to the top of the world, where he would find that the winds had nothing to temper their rage and the wolves were fearless.

40

Bud had hiked about three miles on pavement when the highway finally topped out to where he had good views of Dawson City and the Yukon and Klondike rivers. He took off his pack, already tired, and contemplated his decision.

The winds seemed to have died down some, and he knew that this was a sign that the storm front had arrived, and even though there was no moisture yet, he could see fog settling over Midnight Dome in the distance. He could also see that the pavement turned to gravel and would be muddy if it did rain or snow.

He sat down to catch his breath, taking out a small tin of peppermints he'd bought at the general store in Dawson, the sugar reviving his energies somewhat.

He wondered if he were to turn around if he would be able to catch the ferry on its last run. It could be worth a try, but if it had already made that last crossing, he would just have to climb back up the highway again, and he'd just be that much further behind.

Soon rested, Bud got back up and resumed walking. The highway appeared to follow the crests of rounded mountains across a landscape unlike anything he'd seen before, through large forests of stunted black spruce and low brush.

Now that he'd climbed up out of the river valley, he could see forever, and as he climbed even more he started seeing snowbanks along the road, which he knew could provide him water when needed. Patches of ripe blueberries lined the highway, which was now starting to erode into potholes and washboards.

But what struck him most was the overwhelming feeling of wilderness, of walking along a narrow strip of questionable civilization through almost impenetrable bush and muskeg, a world that was inhospitable to his own species but home to many others, a world that was as foreign to him as the desert back home would be to the large herds of caribou that migrated through here every spring and fall.

And as Bud walked along, he thought about everything he'd seen and done since leaving home. He thought of how the Stampeders had to make over 40 trips across the grueling Chilkoot to carry their ton of supplies, and of how it must have felt to want something that badly, most of them never making it back home, yet alone finding riches.

He thought of how he'd come to a place he didn't know to help someone he barely knew, and he wondered if he'd made a poor decision in doing so, one that might cost him his life. And he thought of Wilma Jean and the dogs, and then of Lindie.

He thought of things like glaciers and dire bears, and then of what a magical yet raw place he was in, surrounded by beauty, and he knew what it felt like to be feral, removed from all comforts. And then he thought of the Lost Patrol, and how Dougie also seemed lost in a profession that didn't really suit him, and how that had impacted other lives, especially Shorty's.

Bud figured he'd come about eight miles when he reached a rest area with tables and an information sign about the Top of the World Highway. He was tired and decided this would be a good place to spend the night. He set up his tent and got ready, then sat at a picnic table, softly playing his harmonica.

And as the night got colder and colder, Bud thought back to the balmy summer nights down on the farm near Green River, listening as the crickets began their evening chirping while the last rays of sunlight faded into the far distance over the San Rafael Swell.

He recalled Old Man Green, though he was at the time just Mr. Green, telling him how to tell the temperature by the number of chirps per minute, though he'd long forgotten the formula. He'd have to ask him next time he saw him again, if he ever did.

He could almost smell the green of the freshly cut alfalfa fields with the distinct wet scent of the river flowing slowly down where the cattails and rushes held the secrets of water lovers such as the big carp that he occasionally would see hiding in the deeper eddies.

And as he sat there, it began—the Aurora Borealis, the Northern Lights, huge hanging curtains of blues and greens and purples wandering across the sky, undulating and dancing. And far far away, he could hear a chorus of wolves howling. With the sky so clear, he knew then that the storm had veered to the south, sparing him.

It was then that Bud knew it had to be a dream—it was all too perfect.

Finally, crawling into his tent, he drifted off, sleeping like a baby, the soft spongy tundra making a perfect bed.

41

Bud was well into his third day of hiking when he heard a sound that was familiar but that he just couldn't identify. Whatever it was, it was coming from in front of him, and as it got louder and louder, his first instinct was to hide in the bushes.

He had almost ducked off the road when he recognized what it was. He was amazed at how quickly he'd forgotten the sounds of civilization.

"Hey buddy, what're you doing out here?"

The pickup carried two men who looked like hunters, both dressed in camo with jerry cans and supplies in the bed of the truck.

Moose hunters, just as he'd hoped, Bud grinned.

"Any chance I could get a ride out with you fellas?" He asked.

"Are you walking from Dawson City? Man, are you lucky. We were just about ready to call it a day and turn around. They're closing the border station this evening. Throw your pack in the back and hop in."

Bud climbed into the back of the extended cab as one guy asked, "Are you a Mountie?"

Bud laughed. "No, they gave me this coat since mine wasn't warm enough."

The other fellow asked, "Did they run you out of the country or something?"

Bud laughed again. "No, they never let me in in the first place. Are you guys from Alaska?"

"Never let you in? Are you here illegally?"

"Kind of," Bud said. "But once we get back into Alaska, I'll be legal."

"We're from Palmer," one guy said, handing Bud a hot cup of coffee from his thermos. "We've been staying in Tok, moose hunting, though this is our last day. But seriously, are we going to get in trouble for giving you a ride?"

Bud replied, "I came in by train over at Skagway and they never checked my passport. I don't think it'll be a problem, but you guys don't need to get involved. Just let me out early, and I'll walk through."

"I'm Thomas, and this is my buddy Paul," the driver said. "We've been coming through Poker Creek for years hunting up here. They won't say anything to you as long as you have a passport. No need to walk through. Where you headed?"

Bud replied, "I'm trying to get back home to Utah. I'm thinking maybe I can fly out of Anchorage."

"We can get you down to Palmer. That's pretty close," Thomas said. "Assuming they don't throw you in jail at the border," he grinned. "Actually, the border agents know us so well they hardly look at our passports. They were in a pretty good mood when we came though this morning. I think they're ready to fly the coop. I know they get pretty bored up here. But were you seriously prepared to walk all the way? It's a long ways to Chicken, you know, almost 50 miles from the border."

Bud was beginning to realize how truly lucky he was. It seemed like ever since he'd got the message to come to the Yukon and rescue Shorty, his luck had held, even when he thought it hadn't. He'd meant to spend time on the Internet at the hotel studying the route he was taking in more detail, but looking for Lindie had taken all his time.

He now wondered where Shorty was, and if they'd released him.

He knew Sue was Dougie's superior, and she'd seemed pretty disgusted with the whole affair, so he suspected Shorty was now out of jail, but he had no way of knowing, especially since Lily and Stan didn't even have a phone. He wondered how Lindie was doing, and if Grady had taken Stan up to Shorty's camp to get his stuff, since he knew where it was.

Before Bud knew it, they were coming around a hill to where he could see a lime-green building in the distance ahead, and he knew they were at Poker Creek. Thomas slowed down, and as they stopped, he and Paul both took off their sunglasses and handed the border agent their passports.

Bud pulled his out, ready, when the agent said, "Nice coat."

Bud handed the agent his passport, laughing, then said, "I'm with the Mounties. Surely you've heard of us?"

The agent glanced at Bud's passport and handed it back, joking, "Of course, everyone's heard of the Mounties. You always get your man. Do you have any illegal poutine to declare?" He laughed, then said, "I have a buddy in the RCMP, and I'd die to have a coat like that."

Now Bud, relieved, took the coat off and handed it through the truck window.

"It was a gift from a Mountie down in Dawson after I helped on a search and rescue mission. It's served its purpose, but to tell you the truth, I'm getting tired of everyone asking if I'm a Mountie."

The agent looked surprised and said, "Are you sure?"

"It may need to be cleaned, but it's all yours," Bud grinned.

"We're not supposed to accept gifts, but since I'm basically off duty in 20 minutes, I think I'll make an exception," the agent said. "What a great way to end the season. Thanks!"

"Where do you go for the winter?" Bud asked.

"The other border agent lives in Tucson, and he's already left. He works the border down there, but I take the winter off. I go home to Salt Lake City."

"No kidding?" Bud replied. "I live in Green River."

"Like they say, it's a small world," the agent said. "And I'm getting ready to close down and go see a bit more of it. You fellas have a nice day, and thanks again for the coat."

Bud nodded goodbye, then grinned at the thought of the border agent wearing his Mountie coat around Salt Lake.

It truly was a small world, he thought as they headed on down the road to Chicken, Alaska, then ultimately to Palmer, where he would give the hunters his camping gear then reconnect with Dr. Curt's parents in Anchorage and fly on home.

42

Bud sat on the back porch of the bungalow playing stick with the dogs, though Pierre would just grab it and chew on it, frustrating Hoppie to no end, who wanted to play fetch.

It had been several weeks now since Bud had been home, and he was slowly getting back into the routine of being sheriff, as well as walking the dogs around the farm and hanging out at the Melon Rind Cafe.

He was glad to be back, and Wilma Jean had seemed extraordinarily happy to see him, proving to Bud that absence does make the heart grow fonder.

After she'd gone on and on about how he'd lost weight, he'd given her the package of Tundra Mud coffee, but she especially liked the jade earrings from the Cassier Mountains he'd bought in Dawson City while wandering around with Lindie.

Bud now felt a pang of sadness, for he still missed the little dingo. He hoped she was doing well, but he was sure she'd be happier with him, especially out on the farm or exploring the backcountry.

He'd talked to Wilma Jean about it, even hinting at going back to Dawson to try to talk Lily and Stan into giving him the dog, but she'd said it would probably be a lost cause, and Bud knew deep in his heart she was right. Lily and Stan had some kind of connection between the little dog and their son, and he knew that kind of emotional thing was never easy to reconcile.

His bag had made it back to Green River, the airlines even having it delivered special courier, as if they'd lost it and wanted to make good, which had made Bud grin.

He'd just spent the past couple of hours going again through his photos from up North, and he had to admit that he'd outdone himself, especially with the ones from Tombstone. He'd already picked out a couple to have enlarged and framed, including one of the bear by the North Klondike River.

Bud was already thinking of how nice it would be to take a real vacation up North, maybe visit the Yukon as well as Alaska, but taking Wilma Jean and the dogs this time. He then remembered what Dr. Curt had told him about how the North gets under your skin and comes back to haunt you at the most unlikely times. He suspected he was right.

Howie had been happy to see him, and it had taken a couple of hours at the sheriff's office to catch Bud up to speed on everything that had happened in his absence, which was mostly nothing. Maureen was doing fine, with the baby growing bigger every day.

After talking with Howie for some time, Bud had pulled out his harmonica and showed him the licks and riffs Grady had taught him, followed by his new song, *The Yukon Trail*.

Howie had liked it so much he was going to put lyrics to it and have the band learn it, and maybe Bud could even play along on the harmonica, which was exciting. Bud then played a moving rendition of *The Ants Go Marching One by One*, but Howie hadn't seemed overly impressed.

It was great to be back, but Bud still wondered if Shorty had been released, and he hadn't had any luck finding out. He'd tried calling Dougie's office, but had been told Dougie had gone back to Alberta, and Sue hadn't been available, as she was up in Whitehorse looking for a new house, now that she was retiring.

Now Bud went into the bungalow, where he poured himself a cup of coffee, putting a dollop of vanilla-bean ice cream in it, then went back outside to the porch, pulling out his harmonica.

Suddenly, from nowhere, chaos enveloped the yard, as what Bud took to be a coyote came running inside the fence, the boys madly chasing it around and around, barking their heads off. Bud jumped up, nearly spilling his coffee, for if the coyote managed to turn the tide and grab one of the dogs, it could quickly injure them or worse.

Now the coyote was coming straight for him, and it nearly knocked him down as it jumped up right into his arms!

Bud could hear someone laughing, a voice he thought he just might recognize.

"Hey, Cheechako!"

It was Shorty Doyle, and the little coyote was Lindie!

Shorty opened the back gate and came into the yard, Cassie by his side, watching as Lindie jumped up in front of Bud over and over as if she had springs on her feet. Hoppie and Pierre were now standing by, watching, as if not sure what to do.

Shorty grinned. "I told you I'd make it worth your time if you came up and helped me, Bud."

"But how did you get Lindie?" Bud asked, still in shock, the little dingo now at his feet, guarding him from Hoppie and Pierre, who looked confused.

"I went to the Klondike Cafe to get my truck and stuff after they released me, and Lily told me to take Lindie, as she knew I was coming back to the States," Shorty replied. "Here's a note for you."

Dear Bud,

Please give Lindie a good home and send us a photo once in awhile. And thanks for the gold mine. That was awfully nice of you.

Love,

Lily, Stan, Joe, Helen, and Grady

Shorty continued, "Lily told me Lindie pined away without you, and they realized it was for the best for her to be with you. Grady's helping work the mine, and he told Lily she was being selfish, which didn't set well, but then she thought about it and had to agree he was right."

Shorty continued. "I got Lindie all her shots and sailed though the border patrol at Roosville at the Montana border with nary a problem. She acted like she knew where we were going, and I've never seen a dog look so happy. Anyway, just look at her now. She's home, Bud. She's a Carolina dingo, not a Great White North dog—she belongs down here, like me."

"Are you staying, Shorty?" Bud asked, wiping the tears from his eyes.

Shorty put his arm around Cassie.

"A team of muskoxen couldn't pull me away," he replied. "By the way, Anderson's recovering and will be extradited back to Canada. He's already admitted to William's murder. He left the diamonds in a locker in Skagway, and the Canadian government claimed them."

Shorty paused, looking troubled, but then continued. "But I have something else for you from Lily, a great big Berry Delight pie. We're hoping you'll offer us a piece. And one more gift, this one from Joe's Uncle Walt, who gave you a ride in his truck. He said to tell you you're no longer a cheechako."

Shorty handed Bud a gold baseball cap with the words in blue:

> Sourdough
> Dawson City
> Yukon Territory

"I made out like a bandit," Bud remarked, putting on the hat. "The girls' hockey team sent me a big box of maple-syrup candy and a really nice hockey stick with all their signatures on its ash blade. But is Lily starting that bakery she was talking about?"

"Yes, they left the old Klondike Cafe and moved into Dawson," Shorty replied. "It's kind of sad, another old abandoned roadhouse, the end of an era. Lily went down to stay at her daughter's in Horsefly for awhile, but when she comes back, she's going to start baking again. And they've been finding some gold on that claim you gave them."

Bud replied, "Giving it to them seemed like the thing to do, since that country was all theirs to start with."

Shorty nodded in agreement, then said, "But Bud, I owe you a lot more than a little dingo dog. How can I repay you?"

Bud laughed, "Well, if you knew how much this little dog means to me, you would know you don't owe me a thing. It was a great adventure, and I got lots of fantastic photos. Let's go have some pie and coffee, and I'll show you how I framed that mining claim you sent me."

Bud paused, opening the kitchen door as all three dogs ran inside, then added, "Besides, legally, I never even left the country."

They all walked inside and on to better things.

The SS Klondike on the Yukon River in Whitehorse. Photo by Chinle Miller

ABOUT THE AUTHOR

Chinle Miller writes from southeastern Utah and western Colorado, where she spends most of her time wandering with her dogs. She has an A.S. in Geology, a B.A. in Anthropology and an M.A. in Linguistics.

If you enjoyed this book, you'll also enjoy the first book in the Bud Shumway mystery series, *The Ghost Rock Cafe*, as well as the second, *The Slickrock Cafe*, the third, *The Paradox Cafe*, the fourth, *The No Delay Cafe*, the fifth, *The Silver Spur Cafe*, the sixth, *The Ice House Cafe*, the seventh, *The Rattlesnake Cafe*, the eighth, *The Beartooth Cafe*, the ninth, *The Melon Rind Cafe,* and the tenth, *The Cessna Cafe.* This is the eleventh book in the series.

And don't miss *Desert Rats: Adventures in the American Outback, Uranium Daughter, Wandering off the Map,* and *The Impossibility of Loneliness,* also by Chinle Miller.

And if you enjoy Bigfoot stories, you'll love *Rusty Wilson's Bigfoot Campfire Stories* and his many other Bigfoot books, as well as his popular *Chasing After Bigfoot: My Search for North America's Most Elusive Creature.*

Other offerings from Yellow Cat Publishing include an RV series by RV expert Sunny Skye, which includes *Living the Simple RV Life, The Truth about the RV Life,* and *RVing with Pets,* as well as *Tales of a Campground Host.* And don't forget to check out the books by Sunny's friend, Bob Davidson: *On the Road with Joe* and *Any Road, USA.* And finally, you'll love Roger Dean Miller's comedy thriller, *Bombing Hoffman.*

Made in the USA
San Bernardino,
CA